THE IMMORTAL VOW

RITE WORLD 3: RITE OF THE VAMPIRE

JULIANA HAYGERT

COPYRIGHT

AUTHOR'S NOTE

I hope you enjoy reading *The Immortal Vow*!

Don't forget to sign up for my Newsletter to find out about new releases, cover reveals, giveaways, and more!

If you want to see exclusive teasers, help me decide on covers, read excerpts, talk about books, etc, join my reader group on Facebook: Juliana's Club!

RITE WORLD

Welcome to the RITE WORLD!

The Vampire Heir (Book 1)
The Witch Queen (Book 2)
The Immortal Vow (Book 3)
The Warlock Lord (Book 4)
The Wolf Consort (Book 5)
The Crystal Rose (Book 6)
The Wolf Forsaken (Book 7)
The Fae Bound (Book 8)
The Blood Pact (Book 9)

1

DRAKE

THE SUN AND THE MOON CONTINUED THEIR HIDE AND SEEK game, as if everything was all right with the world. It was hard to believe that over a month had passed since Thea, Luana, Thomas, and I had fled Castle DuMoir. It was hard to believe I had met Thea only two months ago—and that everything had changed since then.

"Here, my prince." Thomas handed me a glass full of blood.

My gaze still outside, on the darkening sky, I took the glass from him. "How many times do I have to say it? You don't need to call me prince anymore. I lost that title when the castle went-down." Thea had brought the castle down with her magic, but it had been my idea. I went back and forth about how smart that had been, but I couldn't change that now. "And you don't need to serve me things or tend to me. You're not my blood slave anymore. You're my friend."

"I know, I know," Thomas said. "It's just force of habit, I guess."

"You're good at becoming material, though." I glanced at

him. His form was still a whitish mass in the shape of his old body, but now it was less transparent. He was also able to stay in that shape for longer. "You've been practicing."

"It's still a work in progress," Thomas admitted. "Just this morning, I dropped a glass bowl in the kitchen. Luana was not happy about that."

The corner of my lips curled up. "I bet." Luana was temperamental, and she got upset and angry easily. Besides, being stuck in bed for the most part of the last month hadn't helped her mood. "We have to cut her some slack, though. She has been through a lot."

"We all have," Thomas muttered.

We all had been through too much.

Thomas had been killed and was now a ghost, stuck in this world. Luana had been betrayed by her pack and left for dead. Thea had found out she was the witch queen, but she had lost her coven's heart to Princess Morda, who seemed intent on killing Thea.

As for me, I had killed Alex, the bastard who had ruined the DuMoir coven, but now the castle was gone and the vampires were either dead or scattered.

We had fled out of necessity, but we were gearing up to fight back.

"How's Thea?"

I sighed. "She woke up better this afternoon."

"Still no idea what she has?"

I shook my head. Since we came to this house almost five weeks ago, Thea had been feeling sick. She was weak and dizzy and sleeping a lot. "I'd bet all my fortune that Princess Morda put a curse on her before we fled the castle." That had to be it. Thea had already cast every spell she could think of. There was no sign of a curse or internal injury. There was nothing visibly wrong with her. But if Princess Morda had cursed Thea, that could have gone unnoticed. "I'm hoping this person Luana knows will be able to tell us more about it. And fix whatever is wrong."

"So Thea is coming?"

"She wants to." I hoped she would still feel well when it was time to leave.

Thomas's shape flickered. "I'm just so tired of waiting."

"I know, but there was nothing we could do until now." We would have met Luana's friend sooner, if we could, but Luana had been badly injured when we fled the castle. Even with her werewolf healing and Thea's healing spells, it had taken her a month to recover—and she wasn't fully healed yet.

But like us, she was tired of waiting.

The sun dipped, and the orange sky was transitioning to blue. Sometimes, the world outside seemed like a foreign country, a distant planet, a fantasy movie we weren't a part of.

I had thought about giving everything up many times. I knew Thea had thought about it too. But it wasn't that simple, not anymore.

"I can't wait to get this over with," Thomas said in a low voice. "Once we win this fight, this war, I can focus on my own problem." He glanced down at his hands. "I can find out who killed my parents and be free."

My gut twisted.

I could end his misery right now. I could give him peace right this instant. But every time I opened my mouth to tell him, the words wouldn't come out. I had practically raised him. I knew he cared for me as if I were his older brother. What would happen if I told him I had killed his parents?

Would he find peace? Would he leave this world? If he did, it would be with anger in his heart.

I cleared my throat. "We still have a lot to do before that."

"I know." He let out a long sigh. "The sun is almost down. I'm gonna check on Luana."

With that, he disappeared through the wall.

I kept staring at the darkening sky, sure this was some kind of punishment. For what? For being a vampire? For having killed innocent lives? For not telling Thomas the truth since the beginning?

I exhaled deeply. I had done so many bad things in my long life, I didn't even like to remember them. I regretted most of them, though I knew there were times when I didn't have a choice—doing the bad deed had been my only option.

Her soft footsteps echoed in my ears. No matter how sneaky she tried to be, I always heard her coming.

I glanced over my shoulder as she pushed the door open and stepped inside my study. She saw me standing in front of the window and smiled at me. And, like magic, all the regret, the guilt, and the sadness left me. Thea had that effect on me. Whenever she looked at me with so much pride and love in those bright gray eyes, I forgot all the bad, all the dark, all the ugly. Together, we had big plans for a bright future—not just for the two of us, but for all supernaturals.

"Damn it," she whispered, closing the door behind her. "And here I thought I would get you this time."

One corner of my lips curled up. "You'll never be able to sneak up on me."

Walking toward me, she shrugged. "It won't hurt to try."

"No, it won't." I could also tell her that besides her foot-steps, her sweet scent always gave her away. I could smell her even if she was over three hundred feet from me. Vampires had an increased sense of smell, but I believed it was more than that. It was like the pull I felt toward her and she felt toward me. I was sure the fact that her scent was so strong and alluring to me was because of whatever bond we shared.

When Thea was in reaching distance, I grabbed her arm and pulled her to me. I wrapped my arms around her waist and leaned my head on her shoulder, taking in more of her addicting scent.

She wound her arms around my neck. "Hello to you too," she whispered, her tone husky. Desire coursed through me. My fangs elongated, and I grazed their sharp tips over her skin. She inhaled sharply. "What are you trying to do?"

"Just enjoying my love." I forced my fangs to retreat. Even though Thea kept offering her blood to me, I tried taking only a little sip here and there because she had been so weak. It was a relief to hear the stable beat of her heart and see her so strong. I pulled back and looked at her, at her beautiful eyes, at her rosy cheeks, her small nose, her pink lips. She seemed healthy right now. "Glad to see you feeling better."

"It's good to feel better." She stood on tiptoes and brushed her lips on mine. A jolt rushed through my core. "If we weren't leaving soon, I would invite you to go back to our bedroom."

A growl rose from my chest. "Well, we can be a few minutes late."

She chuckled. That happy sound hit me hard. Hell, how I loved seeing her happy. I closed my hand around her nape and crushed my mouth on hers. She didn't resist. She never did. Instead, she opened her mouth to me and let me take all I wanted and more.

Without breaking the kiss, I pushed her back until her legs hit the desk. Taking my time, I slid my hands down her shoulders and her back, grabbed her waist, and pulled her up the desk. She sat down on top of the desk and wrapped her legs around my waist. And I stepped into her, pressing my body into hers even more.

I leaned down, determined to have her right here, right now.

I was about to rush to the door to lock it, when I heard a new set of footsteps approaching.

Breathing heavily, I broke the kiss and rested my forehead on Thea's. "Hell."

"What happened?" she asked, sounding as out of breath as I was.

"We have company."

I took a large step back and inhaled a lungful of fresh air to calm myself down before our company burst into the room. But Thea's scent was everywhere, and it was hard to calm down when she was staring at me with puppy eyes.

I groaned.

A knock came from the door, two second before it was pushed open.

Luana stuck her head inside. She offered us a sly grin. "I hope I'm not interrupting anything."

She had werewolf hearing. She damn well knew she was interrupting something. "What do you want?" I barked.

Thea frowned. "Drake!"

Luana jerked her chin to the window. "The sun is down. It's time to go."

2

THEA

THE FIRST TWO HOURS INTO OUR TREK THROUGH THE FOREST, I was fine. Great, actually. I hadn't felt this good in almost a month. Perhaps I had used too much of my power during the last battle and only now my strength was returning. Perhaps it was the fresh air and the gentle exercise.

But, like a switch had been turned, the dizzy spells began again. I tried to hide them really hard, but there wasn't much I could hide from a vampire and a werewolf.

Drake reached for me. He grabbed my hands and tugged me forward, to keep up with them. "Is it too bad?"

"No," I lied. I channeled my magic, hoping I still had enough to fight this fatigue, this bone-deep exhaustion, but only a flicker answered. Holding on to it only made me more tired.

"You're almost as pale as me," Thomas said in a light tone.

Drake shot him a glare. "Was that supposed to be a joke?"

Thomas's eyes bugged. "Well, yes."

"That was—"

I squeezed Drake's hand. "Stop nagging him."

Thomas slowed down, staying a few feet behind us. The opposite of Luana who charged ahead with her powerful legs. Wearing brown leather pants, a beige tunic, and a leather bandana across her forehead, she looked every bit like a wolf princess. She was pretty too, with her long, light brown hair pulled back into a tight braid, brilliant hazel eyes, and golden skin. I had seen most of her body when I was healing her—she was lean and hard, with the right curves. Her entire body was pure muscle, a trait from her werewolf gene, I guess. However, as much as she looked like a wolf princess, during the few longer conversations we had during this past month, she had told me she had been one of the lowest ranked wolves in her pack.

She still felt hurt for being abandoned by her pack. Or, like she had said, her ex-pack. She was a lone wolf now. A lone wolf who lived with a witch, a vampire, and a ghost.

It sounded like the perfect recipe for a fairy tale.

Shame our fairy tale was as dark as they came.

My stomach turned, and I tripped on my own feet. Drake cupped my elbow to keep me up. "It's getting worse," he said, as if I didn't know it.

"It's okay. I can take it," I lied again.

Luana paused about twenty feet ahead of us. "We're almost there. Just one more hour and we'll be there."

One more hour of gut-twisting nausea, skull-crushing pain, and black-spot vision. I wasn't sure I could take it.

I sat down. "You guys go ahead. I'll catch up soon."

Drake looked at me as if I had seven heads. "Are you really suggesting we leave you behind? The hell." In one swift motion, Drake scooped me up against him in a tight embrace. Grabbing my hips, he guided my legs, so I wound them around his waist, then my arms around his neck. "Hold on tight."

"I'm heavy," I complained.

He chuckled. "No, you're really not heavy."

He resumed walking, catching up with Luana in no time, and I tried not to be embarrassed by the fact that I couldn't even stand on my own feet. On the other hand, this way I could stay close to my man. I could touch him, and feel the hard muscles of his shoulders, his back, his chest. I could rest my head on his shoulder and inhale his woodsy scent. I could even close my eyes and rest, knowing I was being taken care of.

His arms tightened around my waist. "Comfortable?"

"Very," I mumbled. I didn't want to tell him that the motion of his brisk walk made me even more nauseous.

What was happening to me?

I fought against the queasiness and forced myself to sleep instead—at least while sleeping I didn't feel sick. But, as I was drifting off to dreamland, Drake halted. I glanced up and found Luana by his side, both of them as rigid as statues.

"What happened?" I asked.

"Shhhh," Luana said.

I clamped my mouth. With their superior hearing, they were probably picking up sounds I couldn't make out yet.

"How many?" Drake asked in a low voice.

"I don't know," Luana said, equally low.

A shiver rolled down my spine. "Who is out there?"

Luana turned her big eyes to me. "My ex-pack."

A howl echoed through the forest.

"They are getting closer." Drake splayed his hand on my back.

"Then we run," Luana said.

She took off, and without any warning, Drake raced after her.

Sucking a deep breath, I closed my eyes. The nausea came back with a vengeance, but I kept my mouth closed so I wouldn't throw up on Drake.

We ran for what felt hours, though it hadn't been more than a few minutes. By now, I could hear the wolves approaching us.

For Drake and Luana to want to keep running, there had to a lot of wolves coming for us. If they had been alone, I bet Drake and Luana could outrun them, but with me holding the group back, I was sure the wolves would get to us in no time.

Unless I did something.

"Stop," I rasped. Drake ignored me. "I said stop!"

Drake didn't stop, but he slowed down. He pulled back a little and looked at me. "What is it?"

"I'm gonna block them."

"But you're weak."

"And we'll be dead, or at least hurt if I don't do something." I unhooked my legs from around him. "Now, please stop."

Reluctantly, Drake halted. With worried stamped in his green eyes, he helped me to the ground.

I channeled my magic. I could feel it, just out of range of my fingertips. If I could trick it, if I could taunt it, I knew it would return to me. I knew I could use it again, even if sparingly.

I spun around and faced the wolves running toward us. I lifted my arms and, with them, a thick shield wall rose from the ground, going all the way to the top of the trees. It extended for a few miles, so even if the wolves wanted to run around it, it would take them some time.

The wolves bumped into the wall, they scratched at it. Then one of them changed back into his human form.

"Rollin," Luana said, eyeing the naked man on the other side of the wall.

With a cat's smile, he rested a hand on the wall. I was sure it sent little electrical jolts up his arm, but he didn't seem to care. "You can't run forever."

Luana held her chin high. "I don't plan to."

Drake cradled my hand in his. "How long will this wall last?"

"A couple of hours," I said as a new wave of exhaustion hit me hard. I swayed on my feet and Drake caught me in his arms.

"You shouldn't have done that."

"Well, now it's done." I curled into his arms, wishing I was back in our house, lying in our bed, resting for three thousand years. "Let's keep going before they run around it, or find a way to break it."

"Is there a way to break it?" Luana asked.

"I'm sure there is, but I wouldn't like to be here when that happens."

Drake adjusted his grip on me. "Then let's go."

If I had any magic left, any strength, I would have used it to block the queasiness and the pain while Drake ran with his super speed. I closed my eyes and focused on breathing in and out, on Drake's scent surrounding me, on his strong arms around me—that was the only thing keeping me from passing out or throwing up.

I felt in a daze while we zipped through the forest.

"Here," I heard Luana say. Drake slowed down and fell

into step with her. I peeked at her as she pointed to some long vines twisted across the grass, going from tree to tree. "Once we cross this, we'll be safe."

I frowned. What did she mean?

But I didn't have time to ask. Drake and Luana marched ahead—I hadn't seen Thomas in a while. He was probably saving his energy to show up later—and then I felt it. The magic coming from the vines. I felt it all. How they extended in a wide circle around the clearing and the cottage on its center. How they were some kind of shield to stop supernaturals from coming in. How they had allowed us to pass.

Gently, Drake put me down, but kept holding me. He probably thought I would fall down if he didn't. I thought so too.

I stared at the small wooden cottage and a pang cut through my heart. Even though it was completely different, it reminded me of the cottage where Drake and I met so many times before. And now it was gone. Burnt to the ground by Morda and her inner circle.

"Come on," Luana said, beckoning us toward the cottage. "I'm sure she's waiting for us."

Drake frowned. "Did you tell her we were coming?"

Luana smiled. "There's no need for that."

She rushed around the corner of the cottage. Drake reached for me, to carry me again, but I grabbed his arms for support, and walked with him. Rounding the corner, we found a wide porch with rocking chairs. And sitting on one of those chairs was an old woman with a long, white braid, knitting a thick string of dark green wool. She had many wrinkles around her eyes, but even so, I could feel the magic emanating from her.

This woman was powerful.

The old woman stopped knitting and smiled at Luana. "I've been expecting you. How are you, my dear?"

"I'm doing okay." When Luana approached, the old woman stood and embraced her. This woman was tricking us. She looked old, but her movements and her posture were of someone with a lot of energy. She wasn't as old as she looked. Luana gestured toward Drake and me. "I've brought some friends to meet you."

"I know," the old woman said, turning her attention to us. "I've been expecting all of you." Her brows curled down. "Where's the ghost? I could have sworn there was a ghost with you?"

How did she know that?

"He'll be here soon," Luana said. Then, she glanced at us again and her next words changed everything. "Drake, Thea. This is Bagatha. Former Queen of All Witches."

3

DRAKE

I had no idea what Queen of All Witches meant, but by Thea's reaction—her heart skipped a beat, then began hammering against her ribs—I would guess it was either really good or really bad.

"That's impossible," Thea whispered, her eyes wide. "The Queen of All Witches is a character from stories older witches tell to scare little girls, to make them behave."

Bagatha let out a deep laugh. "Scary? Me? No, my dear, I'm not scary. Not anymore."

"What does that mean?" I asked, not liking how uneasy Thea felt right now.

Bagatha opened the door of her cottage. "Come in. We can talk while having some tea." She disappeared inside the cottage.

I turned to Luana. "Who is this woman?"

"I just told you," she said. "Bagatha, former Queen of All Witches."

"Is that even a title, or some lie she told you?"

Luana rolled her eyes. "Drake, lose the attitude.

Remember I told you she probably knows about your bond." With that, Luana entered the cottage.

Beside me, Thea was still frozen in the same spot. "What is it?"

"I ... I don't know," she whispered. "I can feel the magic pouring out of her, but I don't know. Queen of All Witches? That was a myth, a legend."

I took her hands in mine and made her face me. "Do you want to leave? Just say the word and we'll leave right now."

She glanced toward the cottage's door, then returned her gray eyes to mine. "I'm just stunned. We're all right. I think she's all right. Besides, what other choice do we have? We need to talk to this woman."

I leaned into her and pressed my lips to her forehead. Her hands squeezed mine. "All right. But stay close to me."

A small smile spread on her lips. "When don't I?" She stood on her tiptoes and pressed her lips to mine.

A sigh ripped out my throat. This woman ...

I put Thea's hand on the crook of my arm and walked in the cottage with her. As expected, the inside was small and simple—a living room with a stone fireplace and two ragged couches, a wooden table for four, and a small kitchen to the side. In the back, an archway led to what looked like a bedroom and bathroom.

"Please, sit down," Bagatha said from the kitchen. Luana was in there helping her.

Thea and I took one of the couches. A minute later, Luana brought over a tray and placed it on top of the small coffee table between the couches.

She grabbed a mug and handed it to Thea. "Bagatha said this one is for you."

Thea wrapped her hands around the steaming mug, but didn't drink it. "What is it?"

"I've put some herbs in it that help with tiredness and nausea," Bagatha said, coming to the living room. "Here." She handed me a dark glass. "Blood from a deer."

I frowned. "Do you always carry blood with you?"

Bagatha laughed. "Of course not, dear. I knew you were coming, so I went out and collected some. It's from this morning, so it's not fresh, but I hope that's okay." She sat down beside Luana and took a mug for herself. "Now, what do you want to know first? About me being the Queen of all Witches, or about your bond?"

I stared at Luana. She raised her hands, palms out. "I didn't tell her anything. I swear."

"If you really are the Queen of all Witches, then nobody would have to tell you anything," Thea said. "Start with that."

Bagatha glanced down at the mug in her hands. "We have been at war with vampires and werewolves and fae, and all other kind of supernaturals for many millennia now. Not to mention with hunters too. Ever since the beginning of time, really. And, as wolves know well, our strength lies in groups. So, the witches on this side of the world got together and created the most powerful coven ever. And I was the witch queen." Did that mean she had been alive for thousands of years? And here I thought she was younger than she looked. "As the war with each species went on, the witches started bickering among themselves—about everything, but the main topic was on how to defeat the other supernaturals. The witches were killing each other. So, trying to prevent a war within my coven, I separated them into factions—the Blackmarsh, the Bluemoon, the Silverblood, the Wildthorn, and the Bonecrown. I appointed a leader for each of these covens, while I became the queen of all witches. We had a common council and periodic meetings so I could check on how each coven was doing." She sighed. "My plan backfired. Separated like that, the covens became enemies. Besides the war with other supernaturals, the witches were now at war with each other. Many, many witches died, and even with all my power, I couldn't stop them. The leaders of each coven now called themselves witch queen, and they created ranks with princesses and councils inside their own covens." She took a sip from her tea before continuing. "In a last attempt to bring peace between the covens, I poured half of my power into the five witch queens, hoping that with that much magic they would be satisfied, they would forget about fighting with the other covens, they would realize they were equals, and they would turn toward the vampires and were-wolves ... But once again, it backfired. The witch queens turned against me. They used my power to banish me. That was over a thousand years ago." She gestured to the cottage. "And here I am. Living in exile in a small corner of the world."

Was Thea buying all of that? For all I knew, this woman could be an old witch who had gone crazy.

"In the stories, the Queen of All Witches had an actual wand," Thea said.

"Oh, yes." Bagatha twisted her hand and a long black stick appeared in her open palm.

Thea stared at wand. "This is incredible. Does it work?"

"No, my dear. It was always only for show." Bagatha pointed the wand to the fireplace. Fire roared to life. "I never needed it."

So, this was for real? This old woman was really the Queen of All Witches? And she had been banished over a thousand years ago ... that was why I had never heard about her before.

"In the stories I was told when I was little," Thea began, "you were depicted as the devil. You stole magic and tortured witches who misbehaved."

A sad smile appeared on Bagatha's lips. "I didn't think they hated me that much."

"Perhaps they don't," Thea said. "They just took advantage of your banishment and created such a nasty tale to scare us."

"It makes sense." Bagatha nodded.

"How about you two?" I pointed to Luana and the old witch. "How did you two meet?"

"That was what, twelve years ago? Maybe thirteen?" Luana glanced to Bagatha. "That doesn't really matter. I had always been fascinated with the scouts in my pack. I wanted to be one. Once, when I was still little, I watched their training in the woods, and after they were done, I tried it out. And I got my paw stuck in a bear trap."

"I heard her howls," Bagatha said.

"But aren't you banished?" I asked.

"I am, but that means I was cast away from the witch covens. I can still go anywhere I like, as long as I don't go near the covens," Bagatha explained. "Besides, Luana was close. I didn't have to go too far. I brought her in and healed her paw."

"And we've been friends ever since," Luana said with a smile. "Bagatha told me who she was when I met her, but because I like and trust her, I haven't told anyone about her."

"Until now," Thea said, her voice low.

I paid attention to her. Her breathing was growing

shallow and her hands were shaking. "Are you okay?" Stupid question, I knew she wasn't okay.

Thea smiled at me, but I could see her eyes weren't focused. "I'm fine."

"The hell you are," I snapped. She always told me she was fine, even when she wasn't. She lied to me about it all the time. It drove me mad.

Her heartbeat sped up. "You're right. I'm not." She closed her eyes and her hands dropped like jelly. I caught her in my arms before she fainted and slid down the couch.

I held her tight against me and stared at Bagatha. "Since you're the Queen of All Witches, then you're probably powerful. Can't you reverse this curse?"

Bagatha's brows knit together. "Curse?"

"Yes. I think Princess Morda from the Silverblood put a curse on Thea."

A loud cackled echoed through the cottage. My anger rose and my fangs elongated. "What's so funny? Can't you see she's sick? Help me?"

Bagatha's laughter faded, but a smile stamped her face. "It's not a curse, my dear. It's the baby."

I froze. "W-what?"

"Thea is pregnant."

4

___

THEA

I stared at the old woman seated in front of me. I was sure I hadn't heard her right.

"E-excuse me?"

Her smile widened. "You're carrying Drake's child."

"Really?" Drake asked, high-pitched. There was a faint grin across his lips, and his green eyes were wide in surprise. It was a surprise all right, but while Drake seemed pleased, I felt shocked and unsure of my feelings.

During my last few weeks with the Silverblood coven, Princess Morda had ordered all our witches to get pregnant. She thought it was the only way to produce a new witch queen for our coven. So, I had made love to Drake, wishing I would get pregnant, but it was mostly for survival. Princess Morda would have killed the witches who didn't conceive.

I never expected it to happen. Witches didn't get pregnant easily, and ninety-nine percent of vampires were sterile. It should have been nearly impossible for me to get pregnant, and yet ...

"That's not possible," I whispered.

"Improbable, but not impossible," Bagatha said. She pointed to the mug in my hand. "That's more than a simple tea to help you with your pain and weakness, my dear. It's a tonic that will grant you a little energy too." She glanced from me to Drake, and back to me. "In any case, even if it's impossible or not, it was meant to be."

"What do you mean?"

Her smile lost its shine. "You're not the witch queen of the Silverblood coven, Thea. Your daughter is." I put my hand on my stomach. It was a girl. Drake and I were having a girl. Drake's hand slipped over mine, and he held on, as if he wanted to cradle the baby in my womb. I shook my head. By all that was sacred, I was pregnant ... "More importantly, your daughter isn't only the witch queen of your coven. She's powerful. She's the new Queen of All Witches and she's the one destined to bring all the covens back together."

"W-what?" That was too big of a burden for such a small baby. "But ... I was able to summon the heart's power before."

"That's because you conceived this child two months ago, when you first met Drake," she explained.

"Even before Princess Morda's order," Drake said.

"Like I said, it was meant to be." Bagatha nodded. "I can feel my magic fading as hers grows stronger. She's getting ready to replace me."

I frowned, feeling a little embarrassed. How did she know so much? Did she have a crystal ball? Did she watch us all day? All night? "Is there anything you don't know?"

"Oh, there's plenty." Bagatha waved me off as if I had told her a joke. "But in this case, I know a lot. For example, I know your daughter became this powerful because of the strength of your bond. The Immortal Vow."

"So we're not imagining things," Drake said. "We do have a bond."

"Yes," Bagatha said. "Some souls are given the gift of choosing how their lives will go, what their destiny will be, and what they want to accomplish. Some rare souls choose mates. You two chose each other as soulmates in the ether even before you came to earth to be born."

"Wait." I lifted a finger. "Drake is five hundred years old. That means ..."

"It means you two chose each other over five hundred years ago," she said. "He was patiently waiting for you to be born. And now you're here."

I glanced at Drake. He had this shine in his eyes, his dreamy expression in his perfect face, as if he couldn't be happier with all of Bagatha's answers.

"I knew you were my soulmate," he said with a lopsided grin.

Bagatha continued, "The magic of the Immortal Vow is so strong, it creates a telepathic bond. I would say you two feel pulled toward each other now, but in the future, you'll be able to read each other thoughts and talk without actual words. The Immortal Vow is a testament of a lifetime of true love."

I couldn't deny this all sounded so romantic and perfect, but there was still one thought that I couldn't swallow. I was pregnant in a time of war. I couldn't bring this child to life right now. It was not the right time.

"I can hear your heart and your breathing," Luana said. She had been so quiet, I had almost forgotten she was here too. "But I don't think it's from excitement."

Drake frowned. He probably heard it too, but hadn't said anything.

I forced the words to come out. "I'm worried. We're planning a war. I can't have a daughter right now."

Drake hooked his arms around my shoulders and pulled me closer. "I'll protect you both."

"Thea is right to be worried," Bagatha said. "But not just because of the battles to come."

"What do you mean?" I asked.

She sighed. "A witch's pregnancy isn't normal. First, it's extremely difficult for a witch to get pregnant, and then it's hard to keep the baby during the entire pregnancy. If the witch is able to hold on to the baby, it's a painful pregnancy, riddled with complications. Then there's the birth. The delivery is long and painful, and most babies don't survive. However, children conceived with the power of the Immortal Vow are so strong, they suck up all the energy around them and end up killing their mother during childbirth."

My heart stopped. My stomach dropped.

"You mean ..." Drake shook his head. "No. No. You can't mean what I think you do."

"I'm sorry," Bagatha said. "But I'm afraid that, if Thea makes it to the end of the pregnancy, I don't think she will survive the delivery."

Drake's arms shook against me. "Thea is strong. She can survive this."

Bagatha looked at me. "You already feel it, don't you? You're already weak. It's because the child feeds off your magic, making you sicker and weaker than a normal witch's pregnancy."

"But ... until a couple of weeks ago, I was more powerful than ever."

"That's because you were able to borrow your child's power to fight back. Now that she's getting bigger, she needs more from you to keep growing." She pressed her lips into a thin line. "I'm sorry, but you'll get sicker and weaker as the pregnancy advances."

Drake stood, startling me. "I can't accept this. There has to be a way to save Thea."

"If there is a way, I don't know it." Bagatha reached for my hand. "I'm sorry."

So, I was going to give birth to a powerful girl who was destined to be the Queen of All Witches, but I was going to die in the process. And all of that while we fight a war. It was too much to process.

Drake started pacing beside us. "We'll find a way. We have to."

"Shush," Bagatha snapped.

Drake halted and bared his fangs at her. "What the hell?"

The old witch raised her hand and closed her eyes. A moment later, her eyes opened. "Werewolves are coming."

"What?" Luana shot up.

Bagatha said, "They've surrounded the clearing."

5

A moment passed before I was finally able to hear them. They waited outside the enchanted vine barrier, for us.

Hell.

"Can you tell how many are out there?"

"Over fifty." Bagatha stood. "I'll buy you some time. Meanwhile, I suggest you run."

"But I thought they couldn't enter here," Luana said, her voice shaking.

"They can't," Bagatha said. "But you can't stay here forever. And they will wait for you forever if it comes to that." The old woman turned to Thea. "Have you drunk all your tea? You'll need its help now."

In a daze, Thea blinked, then brought her mug to her lips. She drank all of her tea before handing the empty mug to Bagatha.

The news of the pregnancy had shocked Thea. When Bagatha revealed she would die during childbirth, she hadn't been as shocked, though, and that concerned me. Wasn't she scared? The old witch didn't know of a way to save her, and still it was like Thea's mind was stuck on the fact that she was pregnant, nothing else.

I let out a long breath. I would worry about that later. Right now, I had to get her home safely. Then, I would do everything in my power to save Thea. Because I would save her. There was no other option.

I hooked a hand under Thea's arm and helped her up. "I'll carry you again."

"No, it's okay," she said, her voice low. "I think I'm fine to run now."

I shook my head. "We'll be faster if I can carry you."

"He's right," Bagatha said. "Let him carry you." She rushed to the kitchen and brought a small thermal bottle and a small note. "Here. Take some of the tea. And its recipe."

I took the bottle and paper. "Thank you. For this and for the information."

"I'm sorry I can't be of more help," she said, sounding truly disappointed. "Now, you should go." She walked to the door. "I'll use my magic on them. When I say now, you run."

Without ceremony, Bagatha opened the door and walked out onto the porch. The wolves howled and growled upon seeing her. I kept Thea and Luana out of view, but I knew they could probably smell us now.

I hadn't given the old witch much credit, but when she called her magic, I felt it. The air sparked with energy, the hair on my arms rose, and everyone grew eerily quiet. She threw her arms out, and a massive wave of magic washed over the wolves, pushing them out and away. A second wave went out, opening a path between them.

"Now!"

I picked Thea up, and along with Luana, we ran.

We ran past the vines and past the wolves, who cried and

howled as they saw us go. We kept running, hoping Bagatha could keep them distracted.

Not thirty minutes later, we heard them coming for us.

And ... toward us.

Luana and I came to a halt when I heard a dozen or so of the wolves coming from ahead of us.

Fifty behind us. Ten plus in front of us.

"What now?" Luana asked, looking around. We were atop a small hill with the trees close together, but none of the wolves were that near yet.

"I'm out of ideas," I said.

"We just fight? I don't think we can take sixty wolves by ourselves."

"I can help," Thea croaked. "Put me down, and I'll do what I can."

I groaned. "I'll probably have to put you down so I can fight, but you are in no condition to help."

"I have to try."

I gently dropped her to the ground and knelt beside her. "Listen to me. We just learned a great deal, and I know you're confused, but you have to think of our daughter right now." I placed my hand on her belly. Hell, I still couldn't believe my daughter was inside Thea. I couldn't explain, but I suddenly loved Thea even more, as if that were possible. "Please, just stay back. And if things go bad ... you run. Just run." I didn't want to think of Thea in her state running from wolves. "Promise me. Promise me that if things go bad, you'll flee."

Thea lifted her chin, but she didn't answer. Hell. I was about to beg her to promise me when I smelled them.

"They are here," Luana said in a low voice.

"I know."

As the wolves stepped closer and into our line of sight, Luana hastily took off her clothes and shifted into her wolf.

The wolves came at us. Thankfully, our spot at the top of the hill, surrounded by trees, was advantageous. The wolves couldn't come at us all at once. Luana and I were able to fight them off for a while.

But they had numbers and didn't stop coming.

One sneaked past me and lunged for Thea. She lifted her hand as if she was about to cast a spell, but instead, she curled into herself, gritting her teeth. Pain. She was in pain.

Panic rose in my chest as the wolf put his claws on her. I moved to her, but halted when pain shot down my arm—a wolf had bitten me. Then another bit my leg, and a third one lunged at my back.

I fell to the ground and several wolves pinned me down. I roared, angered that I had been distracted. Raging for not being able to move and save my love.

I glanced to the side, and as I expected, Luana was in the same situation I was.

One of the wolves on Luana turned into his human form. Naked, he sat on her hips and leaned over her. "Traitor. You're a traitor and you'll die like one." He spat on her.

Still in her wolf form, Luana jerked, trying to get rid of the wolves pinning her down, but that only made them hold her tighter—and bite her.

We were losing.

A new wave of horror filled my core as more wolves advanced on Thea. She raised her hand to use her magic, but only a small spark shot out of her palm. Her eyes widened in terror as she scooted away from them.

The wolves transformed into their human forms.

"Careful. She's a witch," one said.

"Can't you see she's weak? Just grab her," another said.

"She can't fight the five of us," another said.

Thea fought against them, but she was no match for five of them when they grabbed her arms and legs. She screamed.

Panic surged through my body. "Thea!" I cried. The wolves dragged Thea away. "No!" I groaned, summoning my remaining strength. "No!" With all my might, I jerked under the wolves. I was strong, but wounded and outnumbered, I couldn't do much.

Giving up wasn't an option, though.

A roar ripped through my throat, and I was able to push a couple of wolves back. I started getting up, ready to attack the others and run after my love, when a handful of other wolves pushed me back down.

One of them bit my shoulder, and burning pain spread through my neck and arm. I gritted my teeth, not caring about the pain. What I cared about was Thea and my daughter, and they were being carted away from me.

Only hell knew what these wolves would do to Thea. Would they even care she was pregnant? I doubted it. Having a child would be one more reason to get her killed.

I couldn't allow that.

I couldn't.

Through the pain, through the exhaustion, I reached up. I buried my fingers into a werewolf's chest and pulled out his heart. The limp body fell over me, but I kept my arm raised so the others could see what I had done.

They wanted to mess with me? They would all end up dead!

I pushed the body aside, sat up, and grabbed the neck of the next wolf. He whimpered as squeezed his neck until it snapped. The wolves growled at me.

"You think you scare me?" I yelled, a bit of a growl in my words.

A wolf lunged at me. I spun my torso out of reach, but put my arm out, grabbing him by the neck.

A wolf transformed into his human form. "Stop or I'll tell them to kill your witch."

My hand tightened around the wolf's neck. "If you didn't want her alive, you would have killed her already."

That worried me. Why did they need Thea? Did they need me too? And Luana? Where was Luana?

I found her in the same state as me. Pinned to the ground, with several wolves holding her down.

Hell. I needed a plan. I needed to buy some time so I could come up with a plan. How to stall? How to save myself, Luana, and Thea? How to win against sixty wolves?

A bright red light encased the forest, and I closed my eyes for a moment. When I opened my eyes, I saw a figure standing over the top of a hill, sending red magic bolts toward the wolves. The bolt exploded upon contact, leaving a nasty charred wound in its place.

The wolves advanced on the figure, but the red light shone, pushing the wolves back. Then another round of red bolts came. In a matter of minutes, the wolves started howling.

I watched as the wolves retreated.

What the hell?

Before I could worry about the stranger, I had to find Thea. I had to make sure she was all right.

I pushed to my feet and turned toward where I had last seen Thea. The figure was now by her side, extending his hand to her. My breath caught, and ignoring the pain and numbness in my body, I ran to her.

Thea embraced the figure and I halted in my tracks.

"It's so good to see you," she said. Then, she saw me and beckoned me to approach them. Wary, I walked up to them.

The figure pulled down the hood of his long jacket and grinned at me. "Hello, Drake."

6

THEA

Keeran didn't object when Drake reached for me and wrapped a possessive arm around my waist.

Exhausted, I leaned into Drake. Although I had a lot on my mind, I was glad to see Keeran. He looked a little bedraggled. His dark brown hair was longer and messy, stubble covered his jaw, and dirty, ripped clothes hung from his frame. The only intact piece of clothing was the thick, black leather jacket that went down almost to his knees.

I tried smiling, but I was sure it looked more like a grimace. "It's good to see you."

"Yes, you saved us," Drake said. "Thank you."

Keeran opened his mouth to say something, but then his eyes wandered to where Luana had just shifted into her human self. She grabbed her clothes from before and put them back on.

All the while, Keeran stared.

I cleared my throat. "What happened? Where were you?"

Drake stepped up. "It would be great to catch up, but we

need to move. You're hurt and tired, and if we don't move, we'll be easy targets for more attacks."

I turned to glare at Drake when I saw the bites on his arms and legs. "You're the one hurt."

Luana limped to us. "Me too." Blood dripped down her shoulders. "I want my bed."

I looked from Drake to Keeran. "Come with us." Drake tensed beside me. "We can talk more after we've all showered and cleaned our wounds."

I knew Drake didn't trust Keeran, but I did. And if Drake would give him a chance, I knew he would too eventually.

Keeran exchanged a quick look with Drake, and then nodded. "It would be good to wash properly for once."

BACK AT THE MANSION, WE FOUND THOMAS WAITING FOR US.

"I couldn't summon my energy to reappear," he had explained. "And when I did it, I couldn't find you. So I came back and waited."

It was okay. Besides missing what Bagatha had told us, it wasn't as if he could help much in a fight. But he did look frustrated over not being there. We all assured him it was okay.

I turned my attention to the several wounds on Drake and Luana. I insisted on healing them before we set out for showers, but I didn't have any strength left. In fact, I felt like I would pass out; I was trying to hide it from Drake, who hovered over me and wouldn't allow me to lift a finger. Even if I had magic left, I doubted Drake would allow me to heal everyone since it would take a lot from me.

So, I taught Keeran to make some magical healing salve

and to heal with his power. After we were all on the mend, Drake took Keeran to one of the many vacant guest bedrooms.

We all showered and put on clean clothes. I think I even napped for a couple of minutes while Drake took his turn in the bathroom. He was trying to sneak out of the bedroom unnoticed when I woke up.

"Go back to sleep," he said.

But I wasn't having it. There was a lot to talk about, and Keeran probably had a lot to tell us. Besides, my stomach hurt with hunger.

Drake carried me downstairs and deposited me on the big sectional in front of the fireplace. Like his chambers at DuMoir Castle, the exterior of this mansion was different from the inside. The exterior was a huge colonial ranch, but the interior was modern. Beige leather sectionals and armchairs, glass and metal side and coffee tables, light stone fireplace and a sleek TV over it. In the kitchen, where Luana prepared something for us, the cabinets were white and beige with sand-colored marble counters, a long island, and several beige leather stools. To one side was a breakfast table with eight tall chairs.

On the first floor, there was also the dining room for twelve, a library full of books, a half bathroom, and a second living room. On the second floor, there were Drake's study, my workshop, Drake's and my suite, Luana's suite, and three other empty guest suites—and one had become Keeran's.

Drake placed a throw blanket over my legs. "What do you want?"

The smell of waffles and pancakes and bacon and eggs reached my nostrils. And my stomach turned. "Nothing."

He frowned. "Aren't you hungry?"

"I thought so. But just thinking about food makes me nauseous."

A faint smile spread over his lips. "But you need to eat. If it's not for you, then for our daughter."

A hand squeezed my heart. Our daughter. I hadn't had time to process that yet. It sounded so crazy. How could I have a daughter? In this crazy, cruel world. We were at war, for all that was sacred! Besides, I wasn't cut out to be a mother. I had never thought of myself being a mother. Even when Morda had ordered all our witches to get pregnant, I had never really considered it. I had wanted to get pregnant so I wouldn't be killed, but now that I had a baby in my womb, I wasn't sure what to feel.

Drake cupped my face, bringing me back from the dread waging inside me. "Hm, just bring me some yogurt," I said. "And some of Bagatha's tonic."

He placed a soft kiss on my forehead, and then went to the kitchen to help Luana.

A few minutes later, Keeran came downstairs. He looked sharp and handsome with his hair combed back, his face shaved, and wearing clean clothes—a pair of casual pants and a henley tee. Barefoot, he made his way to the kitchen and helped Luana and Drake bring all the food to the coffee table in the living room. I turned my nose and focused on my plain yogurt and tonic. It was the only thing my stomach could handle right now.

Drake sat at the other corner of the couch, with my feet in his lap, and a glass of blood in his hand. Thomas leaned against the back wall, Luana took an armchair, and Keeran sat on another one, across from the low table.

"So ... you're a warlock," I said, remembering the day his powers first manifested. He had been chained to be killed. I was about to act when his power burst, and with my help, he was able to flee my coven.

"That was a surprise to me, too." He wrapped his hands around a steaming cup of coffee. "I'm guessing my mother was able to hide me from Morda? I don't know …"

"You're saying you never knew you had magic?" Drake asked.

"Nope." Keeran snorted. "If I had known, I would have escaped a long time ago."

"And these past few weeks?" I asked. "Where have you been?"

Keeran shrugged. "Nowhere. Everywhere. I've mainly hid in the woods, though I have to be careful with all the werewolves running around." He stared at me. "I heard rumors that you had been captured by Morda, so I was practicing my magic. I wanted to get a handle on it, so I could save you."

A small smile adorned my lips. "If that was the case, I'm sure Drake would have appreciated the help."

Drake stared at his cup.

Keeran extended his hand, and a small red light shone over his palm. It flickered a couple of times before disappearing. "But as you can see, I don't have great control over it. I also realized that when in danger, my magic is stronger. That doesn't mean it's stable, though."

"I can help you with that," I said, feeling proud of him. All my life I had been told there couldn't be any males with magic. No warlocks. They were evil. They would turn against the witches and that would be our end. Yet, here was an example that not everything was black and white. Keeran was a warlock, and I knew he was a good one. His heart was in the right place. And now, with a little training, he could be a powerful ally.

"The hell you will," Drake snapped. "You should spend the next six months in bed, resting."

I gaped at him. "You don't expect me to stay in bed for that long."

"You're weak, you're tired, and it'll only get worse."

"But I'm not an invalid! This doesn't make me an invalid. I can help, I can move, I can contribute!"

I heard a whispered, "What are they talking about?"

"She's pregnant," Luana announced to Keeran and Thomas.

"What?" Thomas and Keeran said in unison.

Warmth overtook my cheeks. I didn't know what to think. Should I be embarrassed? Sad? Frustrated? Happy? This was the most horrible time to have a child.

"That's great," Thomas said. "A mini Drake or, a mini Thea. I would love to see that."

That image turned my stomach, and I set the half-eaten yogurt down. "Let's change subject here." I turned to Keeran. "Since you have been in the woods, what do you know about the werewolves? Which packs are they? What are they looking for?"

"You apparently," Drake said with a low growl. "Since they tried to run away with you."

"Well, I did catch on to some things," Keeran said. "The Silverblood witches teamed up with the Dark Vale werewolves, and they've taken over the remains of Castle DuMoir in a temporary truce. Princess Morda rules as the leader now, and the witches live in the only standing castle quarter. The pack is allowed to roam the grounds and work together with the witches as long as they keep the vampires at bay. The vampires are scattered in the area and are keeping to themselves, feeding on humans as they please. As far as I know, as long as the wolves don't touch a witch, they can do whatever."

"Why would they stay in that destroyed castle?" Drake asked.

"Status," Luana said. "Everyone knows, every species knows that the vampires of Castle DuMoir were the most powerful on this continent. The castle is a symbol. Now, anyone who lives there becomes powerful."

"I get that," I said. "But I expected more from Morda. I can't imagine her living in a caved-in castle."

"There's more," Keeran continued. "Morda calls herself Queen of All Witches now, whatever that means."

I gasped. Drake went rigid. "She can't do that," Drake said. "She doesn't have the power for that."

Keeran raised a hand, palm out. "I'm only telling you what I know."

A chill ran down my spine. I had been sure Morda would want to kill me because I thought I was the witch queen. If she found out I was carrying a child who would become the real Queen of All Witches, then there would be no rest. She would come after me, and she would not only kill me, but also my daughter.

I placed a hand on my stomach. Drake reached over and rested his hand on mine.

Thomas stepped forward. "It looks like Princess Morda is grabbing at straws in an unstable situation. If we act now, we can take the witches and the wolves down. We just need to come up with a plan."

Keeran frowned. "Are you really suggesting the five of us go head-to-head with hundreds of witches and werewolves?"

"If we plan it right, we can pick them apart and deal with small groups at a time."

Keeran shook his head. "I'm not sure you understand me. I just got my freedom. I don't want to march against witches and werewolves and be killed or imprisoned again."

"What other option do you have? To hide?"

"Hey," Luana snapped. "How about we talk about this later." She pointed toward the window. The first orange rays were coming up on the horizon. "We've been up, running and fighting, all night. We need to rest now."

"Good idea," Drake said, scooping me up in his arms. "And you, my love, need double rest now."

I wanted to object, but he was right. I was so exhausted I thought I could sleep for three days straight.

"Good night!" I shouted to the others as Drake carried me up the stairs.

7

DRAKE

THEA CLOSED HER EYES AND RESTED HER HEAD ON MY shoulder. I thought she was deep asleep once I laid her on our bed, but she blinked and stared at me.

"Hey," I said, smoothing her golden hair away from her pretty face. Hell, she was so beautiful, it hurt.

"Hey," she whispered back.

I sat down beside her. "How are you feeling?"

"I'm not sure." Her tone told me she was conflicted. About what?

"I can hear the irregular beat of your heart. Something is worrying you. Talk to me."

She stared at me before saying, "Aren't you worried? A couple of hours ago, we learned we'll have a daughter, a freaking powerful daughter."

I placed my hand on her stomach. "Honestly, I think we're blessed."

She bristled. "Well, I haven't wrapped my head around that yet." I could actually see her struggle accepting this.

"Besides, shouldn't every child be raised by her mother? I won't be here to raise her."

Her gray eyes filled with tears.

So that was the issue. Thea was disguising her fear of abandoning her daughter by pretending to be scared about being a mother, about bringing a powerful girl into this world.

I lay beside her and tucked her to my side. "That won't happen. You'll be here to raise her, no matter what."

She sniffed. "But you heard Bagatha. There's no way to survive this."

"That she knows of." I smoothed my hand down her back. "I'll find a way. I promise."

She buried her face on my neck. "Let's talk about something else."

I kissed her temple. "Like the fact that we chose each other before we were born?"

I felt her lips curling in a smile against my skin. "I think the most amazing thing here is the fact that it all happened over five hundred years ago."

"I've been waiting for you to come to me for a long time," I whispered.

She pulled back and stared into my eyes. "That sounds so absurd, but it feels so right."

"I know." I grabbed her hand and placed it over my chest. "I'm glad you're here with me. I love you, Thea Harrington."

"I love you more, Drake DuMoir."

That was impossible, but I wouldn't keep arguing about it. I pressed my lips to hers, but before I could pull back, Thea hooked her arm around my neck and held me there. She moved her lips against mine. I was at her mercy, always, and I opened my mouth, letting her in. I controlled the kiss, though, keeping it slow and soft. Until Thea straddled me and pressed her body to mine.

"You should rest," I whispered against her lips.

She pulled back just enough to look at me. "I'll rest after."

"But ... I don't want to hurt you."

Thea tilted her head and her golden hair fell over her shoulder like a brilliant curtain. "Is this because I've been weak or because of the baby?"

"Both?"

She smiled at me. "As far as I know, women have been having sex all through their pregnancies."

"But their pregnancies aren't like yours."

"No, they aren't." Her smile fell away. "Maybe it was Bagatha's tonic, but I'm feeling better, and I would like to make love to you before I start feeling weak again. Before I can't anymore."

The emotion in her voice. The glint of unshed tears in her pretty eyes. The rapid thump-thump of her heart. It broke me. Who was I to say no to this beautiful woman who had stolen my dead heart? My soul? As legend had it, she had done all that a long, long time ago.

I lifted my shoulders off the mattress and kissed her—deep, but soft. While I showed her how much I loved her with my mouth, I spun us around and laid her down in our bed.

"I'll take care of you," I whispered against her lips.

A moan rumbled in her chest. The sound hit my core and desire rushed through me. But I had to control myself. I was gonna make love to her, and I would *try* to take it slow and gentle.

That didn't mean we had to stay in bed the entire time though.

Kissing her, teasing her tongue with mine, I held on to her and stood from our bed. I pushed her against the wall, pressing my body against hers, rubbing my hard on against her hips. She moaned. Hell, the little sounds she made drove me insane.

I pulled back so I could get rid of my shirt and her top. Then, I kissed her again, loving the way my chest felt against hers. There was just one thing in the way …

Still kissing her, I snaked my hand up her back and unclasped her bra. She chuckled against my lips while I made quick work of getting rid of that piece of clothing, too. I glued my torso back to hers. Hell, her breasts grazing against my chest was too freaking good.

I didn't want to stop kissing her, tasting her, touching her, but I missed seeing her entire body since she got sick. Now, I wanted to.

I reached down and tugged on her pants. Understanding what I wanted, Thea took over, and I stepped back while she slid out of her pants and panties.

And I stood there, gawking at the perfect woman in front of me. She was freaking stunning. Her breasts were perky and full, a slim waist and flat stomach, round hips, long, lean legs. Desire flowed from every cell in my body, making me hurt.

A blush spread over her cheeks. "Are you just going to stare at me?"

"Hell, no," I said, advancing on her.

I brushed my lips against hers, teased her with my tongue, but then I turned her around. She gasped as I splayed her hands on the wall and pressed my chest to her back, my hips on hers.

I pushed her hair to the side and inhaled, taking in as

much of her sweet, sweet scent as I could. Despite myself, my fangs elongated and I grazed them on her soft skin. I knew she would let me drink from her, but I wouldn't even dream of it.

She moaned as I closed my hands around her breasts. I played with her nipples, rolling my fingers over the hardened buds, and pinching gently. Letting out little gasps and moans, Thea squirmed every two seconds, rubbing her ass onto my hard on, making it hurt more and more.

I slid one of my hands down her stomach to her core. I teased her for a moment, rubbing my fingertips across her inner thighs, then slipped two fingers inside her. Thea let out a hiss and bucked against my hand. Hell, she was so freaking wet.

I leaned my head on her shoulder, planting a gentle kiss on her smooth skin.

"Drake," she whispered.

I felt her core tightening around my fingers. To help relieve her ache, I slid my other hand down and rubbed her clit with my thumb.

That was all it took. Thea leaned back on me as she came, trembling her perfect little body against mine.

I couldn't take it anymore.

As quickly as I could, I took off my pants and adjusted myself behind her.

"Please," she whispered, breathless.

I leaned into her, pressing my chest on her back, and putting my mouth to her ear. "Please what?" I pushed hard around her entrance.

She moaned again. "Please, make love to me."

Letting out something like a growl, I obliged her wishes, and in one powerful stroke, I filled her, going as deep as possible. Her walls were freaking tight and wet around me, and I shuddered.

I kissed her shoulder. "You feel so freaking good."

She pushed her ass back, toward me. "Move," she hissed. "Oh, damn, please move."

This woman ...

Clasping her waist with my hands, I moved. I pulled all the way out and pushed in, hard and deep. She gasped, but kept asking for more. And I gave her more. I pumped into her with all I had.

Her eyes half-closed, Thea threw her head back, surrendering to the pleasure. I trailed my lips along her neck, inhaling her sweet scent. I nipped at her earlobe, and glided my hands from her waist to her round breasts. Her nipples were hard, and I couldn't help gently pinching them. She let out a cry.

This right here, being inside her, touching her, licking her ... it was too freaking much.

I wouldn't last long and I had to. I wanted to.

I pulled out of her and, in one swift move, picked her up in my arms. She yelped, but didn't complain as I carried her to our bed. Then I paused.

Our bed. Our sheets. This woman with her perfect body, and her come-hither smile.

So freaking much.

I crawled over her. She grazed her long nails over my chest and my stomach. Then, she wrapped her hand around me and I bucked.

"You like this?" she asked, her voice low, sensual.

Hell.

I dropped my head, resting my forehead on hers. "You have your hands on me. What's not to like?"

She smiled and pumped her hand over my length once, twice, three times. Hissing, I closed my eyes, surrendering to the sensation. Then, surprising me, she slipped her other hand around my hip and tugged me closer. Still holding me, she guided me into her.

"Hell ..." I whispered, completely gone.

Thea wound her legs around my waist, lifting her hips and pulling me even deeper. I tensed, knowing, feeling I wouldn't last long. I wanted to, but there was nothing I could do, not with her. She was just too much for me.

Thea sank her nails on my back as I thrust into her with long, deep strokes. I felt as her entire body tensed. Knowing she was almost there made me pushed even harder into her. Holy hell, how could this keep getting better and better?

Then, Thea stilled for a brief second. Her walls tightened around me as she came. I fought against it. I even pumped into her a couple more times, but I was a goner. The pleasure exploded deep inside me and took me over. I fell over her, joining her as we both trembled away the bliss.

She kept her arms and legs wrapped around me for a long time, and I dared not to move, lest I spoil whatever was going on here.

After a while, Thea turned her face to mine and brushed her lips over mine. "I missed that."

"Me too."

"We should do this more often."

"Only if you're not feeling sick anymore."

She offered me a small smile before closing her eyes. "Or sleeping."

I chuckled. Her heartbeat and her breathing slowed significantly. She was drifting to dreamland. I pressed a kiss to her forehead. "Sweet dreams, my love."

I COULDN'T THINK OF ANYTHING BETTER: MAKING LOVE TO THE woman who had my heart, then holding her while she slept. I ran my hand through her hair, down her back, still in awe that she was mine. And I was hers. Forever.

Forever.

If she lived that long.

No, I wouldn't think like that. I had to believe I would find a way to save her. I had to. If not for my sake, then for our daughter's.

A daughter.

Thea's naked body was pressed against mine, so instead of resting my hand on her belly, I placed it on her lower back. Thea and I were going to have a daughter. A special daughter with magic. A special daughter that could help us in this crazy journey of making the supernatural world a better place.

I turned my gaze to the window. The curtains were closed, but since they weren't thick, I could easily see the sun setting. Careful with Thea, I slipped from bed, and got dressed: sweatpants and a shirt.

Since we didn't have servants here, or maids and assistants, I didn't have an endless supply of blood. And, with Thea so weak, I hadn't drunk from her in weeks. I hunted in the woods behind the mansion. I usually found a deer or a few rabbits strolling around. I wondered how long it would take, though, for me to drain them all, and then I would have to go farther into the woods, or find an alternative.

But I would worry about that later. Right now, I need to feed so I would be strong for what was to come: finding a way to keep Thea alive through the pregnancy and birth, and the war against Princess Morda.

I glanced at the woman sprawled on the bed. Her heartbeat was steady and her breathing was deep. Her hair covered half of her back, and she hugged the pillow—probably thinking it was me. An urge to go back to bed and hold her hit me hard. But more than that, I now could hear the rush of her blood in her veins, and as usual, it called to me.

Better go hunting.

A couple of minutes later, the sun had set and I ran into the woods.

It didn't take long for me to find a lone deer. I tried not thinking too much as I attacked it, killed it in a second, and drank its blood.

I was so distracted with the warm blood going down my throat, I only sensed him when he was close.

Slowly, I swallowed and waited. When he ran at me, I spun out of the way.

The vampire grinned at me, showing off his fangs. "Playing hard to get, Prince Drake?"

"Lark," I said. The rebel vampire's grin widened. "What do you want?"

"You." He lunged at me again.

8

THEA

THERE WAS NO POINT IN GETTING UPSET ABOUT WAKING UP IN bed alone. I knew Drake wanted to let me sleep and rest as much as I could. Besides, by the looks of it, the sun had set some time ago, so he was probably out hunting. Which was good, because I had too much on my mind, and I hadn't been alone in a while to process it all. But before that, I needed some sustenance.

I put on a simple dress and dragged my bare feet to the kitchen. Thankfully, there was no one there. In silence, I followed Bagatha's instructions and made more of her tonic. Only when that was done and I had taken a seat at one of the island's stools, did I let my mind wander through all the crazy thoughts crowding my brain.

Drake and I shared a bond—the immortal vow.

I wasn't the witch queen.

I was pregnant.

The baby in my belly was the witch queen. More than that, she was Queen of All Witches.

If I didn't die during the pregnancy, I would die during childbirth.

I knew all things connected, like a game of dots, but it was still too much.

Despite it all, I had to be logical here: I knew Drake wouldn't give up on finding a way for me to live, but we couldn't count on that. As far as we knew, I was going to die. So, what were my options here? We could hide until I had the baby. Then, Drake would be left alone to raise a powerful witch. They would have to hide until our daughter was old enough, strong enough, to fight Morda. That could take decades, and the chances of Morda finding them in that span of time was high.

My other choice was to go after Morda now. I could drink Bagatha's tonic and some other energizing potions I knew, and using the last of my power, I could kill Morda myself, before my daughter was born.

The easiest way to do that was to sneak into DuMoir Castle while everyone was sleeping and kill Morda. It wouldn't be easy, but with the right timing and a good amount of luck, it could be done.

"What are you thinking?"

I blinked and turned to see Luana entering the kitchen. As usual, she wore leather pants and a loose tunic over some kind of sports bra. Her long light brown hair fell down her back in a thick braid.

"Nothing," I lied.

Frowning, Luana grabbed a carton of juice from the fridge, a glass from the cabinet, then she sat beside me. "Fine, don't tell me. After all, I'm a traitor, am I not? Who would trust me?"

"Don't say that. You wouldn't be here if we didn't trust

you." I took a sip of the tonic. "Besides, as I see it, you didn't betray them. They betrayed you."

She let out a long breath. "That's how I want to see it too."

"Don't worry. You don't need them. We are here with you. We're like a cool mix of covens and packs. More like a family, really."

She glanced at me, her hazel eyes searching mine. "Since you're family, let me ask you, how are you?"

My shoulder deflated. "I'm not sure," I confessed. "At first, I was shocked I'm pregnant. But now all I can think of is that I'm gonna die and leave this child without a mother." I scoffed. "Which is funny, right, since I barely had a mother to begin with."

"Weren't you close to your mother? What happened to her?"

"I was never close to her. Witches aren't close to each other, outside of ranking. We're raised as if we were in a magical boarding school with severe punishment for each infraction and rule broken." I shrugged. "She was just another witch, though sometimes she yelled at me more than the others because she had birthed me. When I was five, I think, she got pregnant again, but she died halfway through the pregnancy." I paused, remembering those days. "I didn't feel much other than the sorrow of losing another witch."

"I'm sorry," Luana whispered.

"I didn't have a good role model, and I always thought I wouldn't care for kids, because that was how I was raised. Isn't it funny I now want to be here for my daughter? I want to protect her, to teach her, to see her grow?"

Luana's usually guarded eyes softened. "It makes complete sense. You're a different witch, a good witch, and that's why you'll make a great leader."

I snorted. "I don't want to be a leader, to be honest. I just want a better world for all of us."

"That won't happen without a great leader, and I see two in this house: Drake and you. I can't think of a better couple to lead all supernaturals."

My brows curled. "That won't be easy, and as it is, Drake will have to rule alone."

"He'll find a way to save you."

I was sure he would try with all his might. I wasn't sure he would succeed. Of course I didn't want to die, but I would feel better if Morda had been defeated by the time I did. And there was only one way to do that.

"You're deep in thought again," Luana said. "There's something else bothering; I can see it."

I stared at Luana. In the past month, she had been a good friend, even with her explosive werewolf temper. I would dare say she had gotten closer to me than to Drake since we moved to the mansion, even though he had brought her in. If I told her about my plan, would she tell Drake? I had had bad experiences revealing too much to others in the past—Ebby had betrayed me to Morda, and because of her I had lost my coven's heart.

But Luana was different, wasn't she? She had felt the pain of betrayal. She wouldn't do that to anyone.

"I'm thinking about sneaking into DuMoir Castle and killing Morda," I confessed in a low voice.

Luana's eyes widened. Her silence made my stomach contract. By all that was sacred, she would tell Drake. She would let him know, and then he would be all over me like a mother hen and I would never get the chance to—

"Sounds like a good plan," she finally said.

My jaw fell open. "W-what?"

One corner of Luana's lips curled up. "I get it. You're trying to stop Morda now, because once she learns about your daughter, she won't stop. She'll come after you stronger than ever. And the longer it goes on, the weaker you'll be. To have any chance to take her down, you have to act now." My jaw was still open. "I'll help you, but I have a request."

I forced my mouth closed. "What is it?"

"Yesterday the warlock told us the witches are working with the werewolves, which means Ulric is probably at Castle DuMoir with Morda." The glint in her eyes darkened. "Help me take him down, too."

That would be harder. As a werewolf, Ulric had heightened senses, and he wouldn't be alone—his betas would be with him all the time. But ... if we devised a plan to get him alone and kill him, it would be a step ahead in this damned war. Without a leader, the witches, the werewolves, and the vampires would fall into chaos. They would be too preoccupied with each other to find a new leader for each coven or pack, which would give us time to hide in peace during my pregnancy.

We had been fighting for order and fair rules for so long, it actually hurt to consider ensuing more chaos. But it was darkest before the dawn.

After birth ... I didn't want to think about what came then. Not right now.

One step at a time.

And the next step was to kill Morda and Ulric.

"I'm in."

Luana stood. "Then, if you're feeling well, I suggest we go now. Like I said, you'll only get weaker as the pregnancy progresses, and as far as I can tell, Drake went hunting and the warlock is sleeping. They won't be able to stop us if they don't see us leaving."

She was right, of course. I looked down at my bare legs. I needed to change first. Even so, that would take only a couple of minutes. I downed the rest of the tonic and stood beside her. "Meet me in the back in ten minutes."

9

DRAKE

THE LAST TIME I HAD SEEN LARK, ONE OF THE LEADERS OF THE rebel vampires living in the village outside of DuMoir Castle, had been during the last battle.

He and Remi, the other leader, had promised to back me up against Alex and his men after I had lied to them that I would abolish the monarchy, as they wanted, just to get them on my side, but it had backfired. In the heat of the battle, they went back on their word and betrayed me. They didn't want any kind of ruler or rules. They wanted to be free and hunt for humans as they saw fit.

It seemed Lark was doing exactly that now.

I used my enhanced senses to try to locate Remi—I doubted Lark would be here alone—but I could hear anything around us.

"I guess I should thank you," Lark said.

"For?"

"For killing Alex and destroying half of the castle. Everything is the way it should be now." He licked one of his fangs. "So thanks."

I hated when they talked before attacking, because I was sure he was here to attack me. Otherwise, why would he bother? "What do you want?"

"A partner," he said. "Remi was killed by a werewolf during the battle. The others in my group ..." He shrugged. "I don't know where they are. Why don't you join me, and we'll both go hunt for humans?" He glanced down at the carcass at our feet. "It's better than hunting deer, I'm sure."

I was afraid to ask, but I had to. "How have you been hunting for humans?"

"There are quite a few small towns in this area," he said, sounding excited. "There's always someone walking alone late at night. Though ... between you and me, if we got a bigger group, I'm sure we could simply run around town, feasting on anyone who crossed our paths."

My blood chilled. What was this world becoming? Humans would know about us. Did they really think they could overtake the humans? What did they think would happen when they stormed a city like New York? Unless there was a coven of a thousand strong vampires, I doubted big cities could be overtaken that easily.

Besides, it was not right. We were all different species who deserved our space on this Earth. No one was better than anyone. We just had to learn to share.

But it didn't look like Lark wanted to share anything at the moment.

"Look, Lark, I don't think that's right," I said, knowing too well I was aggravating the beast. "For the sake of our species, we need to remain a secret, and for that, we can't attack people."

He stared at me with a puzzle expression. "So how should we feed?"

I gestured toward the deer. "I know things are chaotic right now, but it'll change soon." I hoped it would. "Things will become orderly again, there will be law in places, and we'll continue to prosper ... in secret."

"Are you saying you want to restore the monarchy?" Lark snarled. "You want rules and laws?"

"It's for the best." Otherwise, how would we grow and prepare for a future without rules? I didn't understand why he couldn't see that. "When I get back to the castle, we can come to an understanding. I'll make sure you and your vampires have—"

"That's exactly what Morda said two weeks ago when I went to the castle to check on things."

"What?" That was surprising. Morda was making deals with the rebel vampires? "What did Morda say?"

He spat on the ground. "That woman. I hate her. She calls herself Queen of All Witches now, whatever that means. Did you know the other covens are all riled up and trying to take her down? Morda and her coven are still standing."

"What else do you know?"

"Why should I tell you?"

"Because I need to know. Our future depends on it. The future of all vampires and werewolves and—"

His growl rumbled in his chest before he moved, giving him away. I was ready for him when he charged me. I didn't know what he was thinking. He knew I was older and stronger. He didn't stand a chance.

Before he could touch me, I wrapped my hand around his neck and threw him to the ground. With my hand grasping his throat, I knelt on his chest.

"I don't want to fight," I said in a snarl. "I just want information. Tell me what you know about Morda and whatever she's up to." I squeezed his neck hard. He gagged, but didn't give in. As a show of force, I placed my other hand over his chest, right above his heart, and pressed my fingers down. "Tell me."

He groaned. "All right. All right." I loosened my grip around his neck—just a little bit—and he continued, "Morda is offering to pay anyone who helps her eliminate the rival witch covens. Mostly potions and charms that will help with this and that, but as far as I know, werewolves and vampires have been flocking to the castle."

That wasn't good. "What else?" I pressed my fingers against his chest, hurting him some more.

"She's also paying heavily to anyone who knows about you or your witch, Thea Harrington. She's determined to find you two."

Hell. "Have you been providing information to her?"

His eyes widened. "Me? No? Only lies."

Only lies. Which meant, he had been in contact with Morda and DuMoir Castle. If I let him go now, he would have real information about me to give to her.

Shit.

"I'm sorry," I whispered, before digging my fingers into his chest and pulling his heart out.

I dropped the heart and jumped back, disgusted with myself. What the hell? I was the first to advocate for a good world, a just world, and yet, I was killing a weaker vampire because he might reveal information about Thea and me.

This wasn't right.

But before I could wallow in regret, I shut that part of my brain down.

I raced back to the mansion, eager for a shower, as if I

could erase all the wrongs I ever committed with a simple scrubbing of my skin.

But the moment I crossed the front door, I knew something was wrong.

Keeran was pacing the kitchen, looking impatient. No, worried.

"What happened?" I asked.

He stopped and turned to me, eyes wide. "Holy shit, I thought you all had abandoned me here."

"What do you mean? Where's Thea and Luana?"

I let my hearing do its job, and my breath caught as Keeran said, "I can't find them. They aren't in their rooms, or in any other room in the house. I also looked around the perimeter of the house."

They weren't here. I couldn't hear any other heartbeat or breathing other than Keeran's.

"Where the hell are they?" I said through gritted teeth.

"I saw them leaving," Thomas said, taking form by my side.

I was too worried to be startled by his sudden appearance. "What? Where?"

"Through the back door," he said, his eyes downcast. "Sorry. I didn't mean to eavesdrop. I was just coming in, but they looked so secretive, I remained invisible."

"What else do you know?" I asked.

"Not much. They were talking about being quiet before any of you heard them."

"What do you mean?" Keeran asked.

My hands curled into fists. "Do you have any idea where they went?"

"The only other word I made out was Morda," Thomas said.

Hell. "They are going after Morda."

Keeran's face paled. "That's suicide."

I looked at Thomas. "How long ago was that?"

"At least an hour ago. Maybe two."

"Shit," I muttered. "I can't let them do this."

Keeran dipped his chin at me. "I'm coming with you."

Keeran and I ran out of the mansion and went to save the girls before it was too late.

10

THEA

BECAUSE OF MY CONDITION, IT TOOK US A LONG TIME TO GET TO DuMoir Castle. We hid a mile from the estate and watched. It was dark out, but the waxing, gibbous moon illuminated enough.

Returning here was bittersweet. I clearly remembered the first time I had seen this castle and how I had felt: in awe of its splendor, eager to complete my mission, determined to succeed, and yet deeply afraid of the vampires.

So much had happened in this castle.

And now half of the castle was in ruins. Stones crumbled to dust. All because of me.

"Ready?" Luana asked, bringing me back to our mission.

I let out a deep breath and focused. My body tingled as my magic rose from its slumber, but it remained stable as I cast a weak glamour over us. Right now, when someone walked by us, they would see two witches from the Silverblood coven. However, as I wasn't strong right now, if anyone got too close, they would see right through the glamour.

"Ready," I said.

Unafraid—or at least, pretending not to be—Luana and I stepped out of the bushes and approached the castle. We pretended to be engrossed in conversation to avoid anyone if they approached us.

The maze in the back garden was mostly destroyed, the hedges either torn down or burned. The flowers hadn't been cared for, and the grass looked like it needed some love. I had started destroying this place, but Morda would certainly finish it.

Luana and I stepped into the castle and turned toward the main stairs. If I knew Morda as well as I thought I did, she was bound to have taken one of the main chambers in the castle. But we hadn't taken more than three steps when we heard heavy footsteps down the hall.

Soraya, Morda's right arm, appeared from the end of the hallway. She slowed when she saw us. "What are you doing? The Queen of All Witches requested the presence of all witches in the main dining room." I glanced that way. The ceiling had come down. Was it possible to go through there?

"Hm, but it's the middle of the night," Luana said.

Shit. "And? The Queen of All Witches doesn't have to explain herself to you. Just come along and be quiet."

Soraya beckoned us to follow her.

Luana stared at me with wide eyes.

"We don't have much choice here," I whispered. Weren't we after Morda? If she was in the main dining room, then that was where we were going.

On our way, we walked past the entrance to the main library. There were four witchguards flanking the open archway. For some reason, I stopped and glanced inside. Like many other rooms in the castle, half of the ceiling had come down. The other half seemed supported by tall shelves and improvised stone pillars.

However, it was what lay in the middle of the room's open area that caught my attention.

My heart squeezed and tugged, as if a rope had been tied around it and now someone, something, was pulling at it.

A tall stone pedestal stood in the center of the room, and a box made of dark wood lay on top.

It was the heart. I was sure it was the heart. It called to me.

I placed a hand over my heart as it beat uncontrollably, hurting my chest.

"What are you doing?" Luana asked in a low tone. "We have to go."

But ... the heart. The heart was here. I could take the heart and run before Morda could see us.

Only, that would infuriate Morda even more. If she was after me before, now she would come at me with her entire coven, plus the werewolf pack, and whoever else she could buy. Her fury would be endless. I would have to run from her when weak and pregnant.

Could I use the heart against her? Maybe. Probably. But who knew how I would feel? What if she came the day I was dying? I wouldn't be able to use the heart to defeat her.

Could I use it now? If I was well, I would say maybe. Because we were standing in the middle of a castle filled with witches and werewolves, I didn't think I was strong enough to take them all down.

A man appeared from the side of the room and lazily walked by the pedestal.

Luana caught my hand and squeezed. "Ulric."

I glanced at the four witchguards. "Now is not the time."

But she wasn't listening to me.

Luana transformed into her wolf and lunged at him. The witchguards turned to her.

I just acted. I channeled whatever magic I had and sent a powerful spell at the witchguards. Two were stunned, the other two turned to me. They readied their weapons to hit me back, but I put up a small shield and cast another stunning spell.

The two of them fell to the ground.

When I looked up, Luana was fighting with Ulric, both of them in their wolf form—Ulric a giant brown wolf, and Luana in her light brown coat, not even half his size, but snarling as fiercely.

I raised my hands, ready to stun Ulric, when something flashed in my peripheral vision.

I only had time to twist around and avoid the full blow. A wolf had jumped at me, right at my side, but I jumped out of the way, its claws only grazing my arm.

Still, burning pain trailed down to my fingers. I had no idea who this wolf was, but he was almost as dark and just as large as Ulric. Probably one of the two betas. I didn't care. Right now, I had to help Luana and that meant getting this wolf out of the way.

When the wolf turned around, I was ready. I raised my hands again, my magic at my fingertips. But when he lunged at me, Luana moved too. She turned away from Ulric and jumped at him, closing her mouth around his neck. I heard the loud crack of his bones when she twisted his neck.

I stared in shock.

Luana barely had time to turn away before Ulric was on her again. He rammed into her, sending her skidding away. A growl ripped through his gritted teeth before he charged her again. I flung a bolt of blue light at him. It sizzled his fur, but besides a quick hateful glare, Ulric didn't stop. He scratched his claws over Luana's back, then pushed her to the wall. He opened his mouth wide, and once more I acted without thinking. I shot another bolt at his head. It was a weak thing, but at least it had given him pause.

My hands shook as I channeled more of my power. With a scream, I shot my magic at him—not a weak bolt, but enough to make a grown, strong wolf dizzy, I was sure. But, as the magic flew toward him, Ulric moved. He closed his mouth around Luana's shoulder and pulled her to the side, hiding behind her.

My magic exploded into Luana's back.

"No!" I gasped, horrified I had hurt my friend.

I took a step toward her, but then Ulric snarled at me. I retreated a couple of yards—and halted beside the pedestal. As if drawn by a magnet, I glanced to the closed box over the pedestal.

The thump-thump of my coven's heart beat inside me.

It called to me.

I needed it.

I reached for it. I opened the lid. I sucked a sharp breath at the red mass beating over the black velvet lining. I grazed my fingers on it and a jolt of magic rushed up my arm.

I landed on the floor and hit my shoulder hard. Snapping out of my daze, I blinked and found Ulric on top of me, his sharp teeth and bad breath only a few inches from my face.

This was it.

I was gonna die.

By all that was sacred, I had been so stupid.

Ulric snapped his teeth, infusing more panic into my veins.

A low growl began in his throat and—

"Stop!" My eyes widened at the voice. Ulric and I glanced to the doorway. Ebby stood there, looking regal in a long black gown. She pointed her hand at Ulric. He growled at her. One corner of Ebby's lips curled up, and she shifted her amused eyes to me. "She's mine."

11

DRAKE

WHAT THE HELL WAS SHE THINKING? SHE WASN'T THINKING. She had been hallucinating in some kind of pregnancy stupor or daydream, because there was no way in hell Thea would willingly storm the ruins of DuMoir Castle, which was filled with witches and werewolves, all eager to kill her on sight.

"Are you ready?" I asked Thomas.

I looked up at the place that had once been my home. From our position behind the destroyed maze, we could see half of the castle was gone, the stones broken into rumble. I wasn't sure how to feel. Sad my home of five hundred years was destroyed? Relieved that this place was crumbling and losing its power?

"I'm ready," Thomas answered.

I sucked in a long breath. "Then let's go."

Thomas disappeared. I gritted my teeth as Keeran and I waited.

Two minutes.

Five minutes.

Eight minutes.

I was going out of my mind when finally, eleven minutes later, Thomas was able to light the fire in the fireplace in one of the sitting rooms adjacent to the ballroom and create a growing bonfire. I had told him where to find fire-starters and even gunpowder. Depending on how long Thomas was able to hold his energy, he would be able to spread gun powder through the ballroom and create a huge fire.

But we didn't need to wait for that.

The witches and werewolves rushed out, going for the wrecked part of the castle.

"What's going on?"

"Who did this?"

"How'd the fire start?"

They talked to each other, practically screaming about the situation.

"Now," I whispered.

In the cover of the night, Keeran and I ran into the castle. Once inside, we hid behind a column and I listened.

There was too much going on with the fire outside, and some witches and werewolves were still running out through other doors and openings, but I focused. Thea and I didn't share this Immortal Vow for nothing. I knew I could find her anywhere. If it wasn't with my hearing, then it would be with my dead heart.

I closed my eyes and focused on her. On my love for her. On my desperation that she was probably caught and hurt.

A strong tug practically moved my chest.

I would have smiled in relief, but there was no time to waste. I beckoned for Keeran to follow me. We rushed, being careful not to be seen, toward the pull.

We rounded the corner to the hallway leading to the main dining room and saw four witchguards on the floor.

I forgot all about stealth and ran.

I halted at the door, my blood chilling.

Ulric and Ebby stood tall in the center of the room, holding Thea and Luana cornered against a wall. Thea looked fine despite her condition, but Luana was naked in her human form, curled against Thea, and bleeding. And right at the girls' feet was Rollin's body.

Hell.

"I don't care," Ulric snapped at Ebby. "I want their hide."

"No!" Ebby shouted. "The Queen of All Witches wants Thea alive."

Ulric growled. "Fine. Then take that bitch, but leave the wolf to me."

"Fine," Ebby said through gritted teeth.

Like hell she would take Thea.

"I'll take Luana," Keeran said. "Just worry about Thea."

I nodded. We rushed into the room.

Ulric didn't look surprised, but Ebby's eyes widened and it took her a moment to act. While Keeran ran to the girls and Ulric lunged at him, Ebby gathered magic in her hands and hissed at me. With my speed, I ran to her and shoved her back. She flew into one of the bookshelves lining the library's wall and fell to the ground—with several books crashing on her head.

I spared a glance at the fight beside me—Keeran stood in front of the girls, a shield in between him and the pack leader. Outraged, Ulric rammed into the shield, trying to break it, but the shield held.

With a smug grin, Keeran lifted both his hands toward Ulric. The pack leader's eyes widened, and a moment later, he started squirming and howling. Whatever Keeran was doing, it was causing Ulric a great deal of pain.

"I can't keep him back for long," he told me.

"Then just do what you can and get Luana out," I said, staring at Ebby as she rose to her feet. "I'll follow you in a moment."

I didn't watch, but I heard more howls from Ulric, then Luana's protests about leaving Thea behind.

I felt the crackles in the air as Ebby summoned her magic to attack. Though I would love to squeeze Ebby's throat, I wasn't here to fight. I was here to save my love and my daughter.

The fighting could wait.

I dashed to Thea.

And bumped into a shield.

Ebby cackled. "She's mine."

I bared my fangs at her. "No, you're mistaken. She's *mine*."

I lunged at her.

Ripples of pain assaulted my gut and I fell to the ground. The pain squeezed my muscles and organs like they would pop at any minute.

Ebby strolled to me. "Wonder how I'm strong? Well, I'm not. Not alone." She halted beside the pedestal in the center of the room and placed her hand inside the open box. "But with the heart so close, with me touching the heart, I can do almost anything." She twisted her hand, sending more ripples of pain through me. I gritted my teeth, but it was impossible to not grunt and jerk.

"Stop!" Thea screamed.

Ebby tsked. "Why? This is so much fun. And if I kill him before I take you, the Queen of All Witches will love me forever."

My mind was melting while my muscles were popping. Next, I could see my bones snapping. Then, I wouldn't be able to move, and Ebby would be free to stake my heart.

I had to do something. I had to move. If only I could get to the heart, take it from Ebby, toss it to Thea.

I gritted my teeth and pushed the floor, trying to stand up.

A new wave of pain crashed over me, sending me down like a lead balloon. My breath fled from my lungs, and all I could see was the red of my rage and my pain. It spread to all of my senses.

I was one second from losing consciousness.

A burst of pure power erupted through the room. I regained enough of my vision to see Thea standing on the other side of the room, her hands raised, and her blue magic pushing Ebby back. Ebby fought against it, but like the ocean had closed in on her, Ebby drowned and fell to the ground. She shook, fighting against it, but Thea's magic was too strong for her.

I frowned at Thea.

How was she doing that?

To my surprise, Thea lowered her hands, her knees giving away, and she slid to the floor.

Gathering all of my strength, I pushed through the last of the daze and pain and rushed to Thea. I scooped her off the floor and ran. I didn't look back as I used my speed to go as fast as I could.

While we ran across the garden, I asked, "What was that?"

"Our daughter. She wanted to save her dad," Thea said, her voice weak.

A mix of pride and frustration settled in my chest. I was proud that my daughter stepped in to help me, but I was frustrated because now Thea would feel even more spent than before.

I didn't say anything else as I ran into the forest. The scent of Luana's blood was thick in the air, and it didn't take long for me to find them in the woods.

"She's bleeding too much," Keeran said as I halted beside him. "We need to heal her now, or she'll bleed out before we reach the mansion."

Thea whimpered. "I hit her hard."

"What do you mean?" I asked.

"Ulric used her as a shield and my magic hit her," she said, upset.

Keeran pressed his lips together. "It's okay. She'll be fine."

I closed my eyes for a moment and listened. "The were-wolves are too close. We don't have time to heal her."

To be honest, I didn't even think we had time to continue running. Keeran was a warlock. He wasn't fast like a vampire or werewolf. And he still had to carry Luana, which would slow him down.

We were doomed.

"I've got an idea," Keeran said. "But first, I need to stop her bleeding." He placed a hand over Luana's wound. A red light shone from his palm and the wound closed."

My ears prickles as the wolves' footsteps grew near. "Whatever you're up to, you better do it now."

Keeran shot up. He raised his arms in front of him and gritted his teeth as he summoned his power.

"What are you doing?" Thea asked, her eyes wide.

A small black circle appeared between his hands. Keeran groaned as he opened his hands and the circle grew and grew. By the time the circle was half the size of a door, Keeran's face was red and his forehead was dripping with sweat.

"Go," he croaked.

"What?" I stared at the black circle.

"It's a portal," Thea explained, her voice weak.

I gaped at it for a second. Then, I heard the wolves only a few yards away. Holding Thea tight, I crossed the portal—into the backyard of our mansion.

I heard the cries of the werewolves as Keeran crossed with Luana.

A wolf jumped through after them, a second before the portal closed.

I put Thea down and grabbed the wolf as it lunged for Luana. Enraged and with my adrenaline pumping in my veins, I pinned the wolf down and broke its neck.

I glanced around to make sure no other wolf had come through, then turned to the others. Thea was halfway to fainting, Keeran looked like he had burned his body and mind away with his last spell, and Luana's wound still needed some tending.

What a team.

I let out a long breath. "At least we're all safe now."

I helped them all inside. Keeran to his bed, Luana to the kitchen where she wanted to see what she could about her wound, at least until Keeran was better and could heal more of it, and Thea to our bedroom.

Dirty, sweaty, and with some blood smeared over her clothes, Thea lay down on our bed, too tired to move.

I paced beside the bed, not sure I should open my mouth. Because the moment I did, I would scream at her. What the hell was she thinking? She couldn't put herself in danger like that. And the baby? What about me? What did she think I felt knowing she was out there alone?

When I finally stopped and looked at her, I found her sleeping. The steady rhythm of her heart and her deep breathing confirmed it. Hell. She had been so exhausted from the fight. And using magic like that? Was she crazy?

I sat down beside her, despair growing in my chest. In my long life, I had never felt so lost, so helpless. It was more than running away and using magic carelessly. It was more than caring about our baby, making sure she was all right.

It was about her. Her life.

I couldn't accept that her days in this world were numbered. To me, there would be no life without Thea. She couldn't die. Her daughter would need her. I would need her.

I rested my hand on her belly, still stunned by the fact that there was a baby growing in there. A powerful baby. Our baby.

Light shone from the cracks around the curtain. The sun was rising again. This time, I was the one feeling exhausted. Not physically, but emotionally.

I lay down in bed beside Thea. As if she were a magnet, she turned to me and wound her arm over my chest. A smile spread over my lips. I heard her deep intake and the slow acceleration in her heartbeat before she peeked from underneath her long lashes.

"You're still awake?" she asked in a whisper.

"I'm trying to calm down before I yell at you about the foolish thing you just did," I said, surprised I was able to keep the fury and disappointment at bay.

"I'm sorry." She snuggled her face on my neck. "I'm so sorry."

"I have to ask: What the hell were you thinking?"

"I thought ... I thought I could sneak into the castle and kill Morda before things got worse. Before I became too weak to even get up. Before I can't protect our daughter. When Morda finds out about her, she'll come and kill us all. I can't let that happen. I had to try to do something." She sighed. "But everything was messed up from the beginning. It was the middle of the night, but Morda and the witches were up. They were awake and in some sort of meeting."

"That is strange," I admitted.

"I saw the heart. I almost touched it. I almost grabbed it."

"I know. I saw it too." I wrapped my arms around her and embraced her tight. "I understand you want to save our daughter, but next time, talk to me, please. I can help you come up with a plan, or I can tie you to the bed."

She chuckled. "I'll remember that."

I pulled back and stared into her stormy gray eyes. "I love you, Thea, way more than words can say. Please, don't try any more stupid stuff."

She nodded once. "I promise."

"Also promise me you won't leave anymore. Even if it is to go buy something in the nearest town. Just don't." I grimaced at my words. "I know I sound mean, but I prefer knowing you and our daughter are safe. I'll get you anything you need, okay?"

"Okay," she whispered.

"Do you promise?"

"I promise."

Her words rang true, but were laced with sadness. I tried to understand how she felt. Being stuck inside a house while she got weaker and weaker, grew larger and larger, and just waited for death? It didn't look like the best forecast.

But I would change it. Hell, I would find a solution.

I pressed my lips to her forehead and held her tight, because right now, it was the only thing I could do.

12

THEA

WHEN I PROMISED DRAKE I WOULDN'T LEAVE THE HOUSE, I meant it. But after a month stuck in this place, watching while Drake, Luana, Keeran, and even Thomas came and went everywhere, I was starting to lose my mind.

I got up from bed and looked at my reflection on the floor-length mirror. My hair was messy, but long, much longer than it had been six weeks ago. My always fair skin was ghost-white now. Instead of gaining a few pounds, I had lost some and my bony cheeks and collarbone were there to prove it.

I looked down. From my calculations, I was nearing the fourth month. I could see a bump in my belly now. I rested my hand on the bump. How was it possible that sometimes I still couldn't believe I was carrying a child? My child. Drake's child. A child that would become the Queen of All Witches.

If she survived this pregnancy.

I couldn't complain, though. Bagatha had scared me, but I was expecting much worse. So far, I had just been too exhausted and too nauseous to do anything else other than sleeping and eating when my stomach allowed it.

However, the other residents of this house didn't stop. I knew they were searching for a way to save me so I wouldn't die in childbirth. Often, they came back from a long outing, carrying loads of books. I once asked where they got the books. Nobody answered me, but from what I gathered, they had been raiding libraries all over the state.

But most books were about legends and supernaturals, so I wasn't really sure which libraries they were going to.

I felt so useless beside them. I hated this feeling, that I was a burden they had to deal with. I hated just sitting here and waiting. I hated not being able to help other than reading the books with them.

Last night, while they were all out doing whatever, I had an idea. Finally, something I could help with.

An hour before sunrise, I drank one of Bagatha's tonics to make sure I had enough energy for the argument that was sure to ensue, and called them all to meet with me in the living room.

They had to push aside the books and scrolls—*scrolls?*—spread around the place, but finally we sat down to talk.

"What is it?" Drake asked from my side.

"I had an idea of something we could do to defeat Morda," I said.

He frowned. "Right now, I'm interested in finding a way to save you."

"I know and I appreciate that, but you have to know Morda is probably after us. And we aren't that far from DuMoir Castle. She's bound to find us sooner or later. We need to be prepared." Drake shook his head. I took his hand in mine. "Please, just hear me out."

"Ignore him," Luana said from the armchair across the coffee table. "Tell me."

"Hey," Drake snarled. "You two already came up with a half-insane, half-suicidal plan a few weeks ago."

Luana rolled her eyes. "This time she'll share it with all of us. If you want to stop us, you'll be able to."

"Tell us," Keeran said, serious.

Drake growled at him, but Keeran didn't even bat an eye.

I held back a smile. "I want to contact the Witch Queen of the Blackmarsh and the Bluemoon covens."

"Didn't you burn Queen Sarah a few months ago?" Drake asked. "If you come anywhere near her, she's sure to kill you."

"If I send her a message explaining my intentions before we meet, I don't think she'll hurt me."

"And what is your intention?"

"To get them to join us against Morda."

Drake gaped at me. "Why do you think they would do that?"

"The three covens have been at war for years," I said. "And now that Morda has allied with the werewolves, the Silverblood coven is stronger. Morda might have pushed them aside for now, but she will eventually turn her full attention and power to the Blackmarsh and the Bluemoon. I think it's in their best interest if they join us for this war."

"What about the Wildthorn and Bonecrown?" Luana asked. "Bagatha mentioned they were part of her coven centuries ago."

"The Wildthorn and Bonecrown have moved farther away," I explained. "And the last I heard about them was that they didn't want to be involved with any of the other covens."

"Witches are crazy," Luana muttered.

I hated to agree with her.

"More than crazy, witches are individual beings. No offense," Keeran said. "It would be hard to convince them to join us for a war."

"We need to find an argument and convince them," I insisted. "Because without an army, I don't see how we can win."

"I don't like this idea," Thomas said. As usual, he had been hovering behind us. I almost forgot he was even there.

"I agree with Thea," Luana said.

"Of course you do," Drake snapped.

The way those two bickered reminded me of siblings. Real siblings, not witches or vampires or werewolves, but human ones who bickered and teased and argued with each other, but still loved each other no matter what.

We really looked like an impossible family.

"But she's right," Luana argued. "The five of us, or three if we don't count Thea and Thomas, against a castle full of witches and werewolves? Not to count the vampires roaming around the forest? We can't win. We need an army."

I extended my arm toward Luana and stared at Drake. "Exactly."

"When you put it that way, I have to agree too," Keeran said. "I still think it'll be hard to convince them, but we should try."

Drake groaned. "I guess I'm the only who doesn't like this idea."

"No, you're not," Thomas said. "I also don't like it."

"You don't count," Luana said. I knew she didn't mean it in a bad way, but the hurt was clear on Thomas's face. "Not liking is one thing. You can not like it and still go with it. What is it, Drake?"

Drake fixed his eyes on mine. I knew I had won before he

even opened his mouth to say, "All right. We can contact them and talk to them."

I sighed in relief. "All right, I'll prepare a spell to contact them."

Drake grabbed my wrist before I could get up. "You shouldn't be doing a spell. Let Keeran do it."

I shook my head. "It doesn't take much for this spell, but I need a few herbs to help me with it."

I was sure it didn't make sense to him. Why not just snap my fingers and send a message to the witch queens? Because each spell worked differently. If it was that easy to contact others, a lot of things would have had different outcomes.

I patted Drake's leg before pushing up from the couch and walking upstairs to the guest bedroom that had become a workshop of sorts. Right after buying this house, Drake had stocked the room with all the herbs he knew and didn't know, plus some other ingredients he had heard of in his long five hundred years.

I entered the room and Drake followed me inside—I hadn't even seen him coming behind me. He closed the door and stared at me.

"What?" I asked, going to the long wooden table in the middle of the room.

He ran a hand through his hair. "I'm worried."

"About?"

"Us."

My brows curled down. "Why?"

"We have been arguing too much lately."

"I don't think it's too much, and isn't it normal for couples to argue sometimes?"

He took a step closer then stopped himself. "I just feel like there's something between us that wasn't there before, and I want to fix it."

"I think the something between us is right here." I touched my growing belly. The humor didn't work as Drake continued staring at me with a hard gaze. I sighed. "I know what you mean, and I think the something between us is the fact that I want to help more and you won't let me."

"You know why."

"I know, but whenever I'm feeling okay, I want to help."

"When you're feeling okay, you should rest some more because you never know how long it'll last."

I closed my eyes for a moment. "Drake, I finally found something I can do to help. Please, let's not argue right now."

His hands wrapped around my shoulders. "I don't want to argue. Not now, not ever. I'm sorry if I worry about you and the baby too much. I can't help it."

I stared up at him. "I'm fine. Right now, at least." I rose to my tiptoes and brushed his lips with me. "Relax a little. Smile. Kiss me."

A low growl ripped from his throat, and he leaned over me, taking my mouth with his. He pushed me back until my legs hit the table, and he caged me in, his strong body pressed against mine.

His hold was firm but gentle, unlike his kiss—he devoured my lips, as if he hadn't fed in over a month and needed my blood right now. Unfortunately, I couldn't give any right now, but there was something else I could give him.

I slid my hands down his chest, over his stomach, to his pants.

Drake broke the kiss and took a large step back. "I'm sorry," he said, out of breath. "I know you haven't been feeling well. I should have controlled myself."

He was right. I hadn't been feeling well, and that was why we had to take advantage of when I was. And right now, I was feeling great and turned on by him.

A small smile spread over my lips, and holding Drake's gaze, I pulled my dress over my head and threw it to the floor.

Drake's jaw hit the floor as he stared at me.

"Want to help me take off the rest?" I gestured to my bra and panties.

"But—"

"Drake, don't think too much. Just make love to me. Right now."

One moment, he was staring at me, his eyes darkened, and a low growl rumbling from his chest. The next, he had his hand around my back and his shirtless body pressed to mine.

I chuckled. "Gotta love that vampire speed."

He showed me a smile before capturing my mouth with his. He kissed me soft and deep, and despite my protests that I wanted more, he took his time pleasuring me. He made love to me just like that—soft and deep. Even if I could have lived for a thousand years, I was sure I could never get sick of him. By all that was sacred, I couldn't get used to him either. The way he made me feel, it was like nothing else.

And if I could be granted one wish, I would ask to have this with him forever.

13

DRAKE

THEA ENDED UP NOT WORKING ON THE SPELL LIKE SHE WANTED. After we made love, she fell asleep almost instantly and I took her to our bed. I thought about joining her and holding her, even if I didn't really feel like sleeping right now, but I felt restless. I had been feeling restless ever since Bagatha told us about the Immortal Vow and the pregnancy and what would happen to Thea.

I think I had felt restless before that, because of the war and the chaos falling over our world, but this was different. Whenever it was about Thea, and now about our daughter, it was always different.

Despite the fact that I was sure I had already read all the books we had brought to the house, I went downstairs to the dining room and skimmed some pages, just so I felt like I was doing something.

After a few minutes, though, frustration erupted from my cells, and I threw the book across the room. It skidded down the hallway toward the kitchen. Keeran stepped around the island, picked up the book, and brought it to me.

"I'm guessing it's not going well?"

I groaned. He knew it wasn't going well. He and Luana and Thomas had been helping me. We had exhausted every avenue we could think of to learn more about the Immortal Vow and how to save Thea.

Speaking of which ... "Where's Luana? And Thomas?"

"Thomas said something about recharging his energy and disappeared, and Luana went out for a run."

Luana and her runs. At least twice a day, she went out to run. To stretch her legs and condition her muscles, she had said. It was one of those wolf things I didn't understand.

Closing my eyes, I buried my face in my hands. "I can't ... I don't know what else to do."

"I think I know."

I snapped my head up, my eyes wide. "What do you mean?"

"Last night, I remembered something. A spell I have seen some of the Silverblood witches do before."

"What spell?"

"A summoning spell, but you don't summon a specific person. When summoning, you ask a question, and then the spell will bring you whoever can answer it."

"And it works?"

"Well, the person summoned can refuse to answer, but they always know the answer."

"So we could summon someone who can tell us more about the Immortal Vow?"

Keeran dipped his chin. "Yes."

"Can you do it?"

"I'm not sure. I've never tried anything like that before."

"A few weeks ago you didn't know you could do a teleportation spell."

"Yeah, but I spent a week in bed after that."

"Wouldn't you do that again? For Thea?" I was playing dirty, but I knew he had a soft spot for her. After all, she had been his first friend, the first person who had treated him like a human being, not a slave. And she had been the one who helped him escape. He owed her a lot.

"I wouldn't have said anything if I wouldn't," he said. I let out a long, relieved breath. "But I have to warn you. I've never done it before, and I'm not really sure it'll be one hundred percent correct. Also, I remember the witches saying that we can summon anyone. I can summon a deadly fae, for example, and if that person is stronger than me, it could mean trouble."

"Are you telling me that because you want me to tell you not to do it? Because I won't."

"No, I am just preparing you in case we need to fight whoever comes with the spell."

A growl rumbled in my chest. "I'll be ready."

Together, Keeran and I moved the couch and the coffee table to one side of the living room, clearing up space. Next, Keeran drew a circle on the floor while I gathered some herbs and other things he said he would need for the spell.

After drawing the circle, Keeran mixed the herbs, creating a thick brownish liquid. He sprinkled that over the lines forming the circle while chanting some words I didn't understand.

When that was done, he stepped back and glanced at me. "Ready?"

Standing on the other side of the circle, I nodded.

Red light shone from Keeran's hands as he raised his arms in front of himself. He closed his eyes, focusing on whatever spell he was working on, and soon, red light gleamed from the lines forming the circle.

"Ask your question," Keeran said, his voice breaking from the strain.

"How do I save a witch with the Immortal Vow from dying in childbirth?" My voice was loud and clear. I had put all my wish and intent into my words.

Keeran grunted, as if the spell was hurting him.

I started for him, but before I could give two steps, a form moved in the center of the circle. It started as a black shadow the size of a golf ball. Gritting his teeth, Keeran opened his arms to the side, and the black shadow grew with the movement. Soon, it took a human form.

"Drake?" the shadow whispered, its voice eerie.

But even then, I knew that voice.

A chill ran down my spine. I watched as the form gained color and sharpness, not believing my eyes.

A tall man with blond hair and regal clothes stood in the middle of the circle.

"Lord Reynard," I said, my voice a thin shrill.

"Hello, Drake." Even though he glanced around as if scouting the place, he looked at ease. "Where are we?"

"M-my house," I answered.

"And who are you?" he asked Keeran. But Keeran didn't answer. He was too focused and strained on keeping this spell up.

"His name is Keeran."

"He's a warlock."

"Yes."

Lord Reynard frowned. "I thought the witches didn't allow males to grow up."

"They don't. Keeran only found out about his powers two months ago."

Lord Reynard's shifted his gaze to me. "Why aren't you at DuMoir Castle?"

I shook my head. "As much as I would love to tell you all that has happened these past couple of months, and ask you for your advice in everything going on, I don't have time for that."

Lord Reynard crossed his arms. "Then why did you summon me?"

"I found out I share a bond with a witch," I said simply. "The Immortal Vow. Do you know anything about that?"

He shook his head. "I've heard about it before, but I don't know any details. Why?"

I sighed. "Because she's pregnant with my child and she'll die. I need to find a way to save her."

"I'm sorry, Drake. I really don't know anything useful about the Immortal Vow."

My dead heart shriveled and my shoulders sagged. "Although I'm glad to see you, Lord Reynard, we were trying to summon someone who could help me save Thea."

He pressed his lips into a thin line. "Perhaps I can still help you, but not with that specific answer."

"What do you mean?"

"Tell me, Drake, why are you hiding here when you're supposed to take my place and be the leader of DuMoir Castle?"

"What?"

"Some of Sarki's visions are simple, but some of them are intricate and specific," he told me. "A long time ago, she had one of those visions and it was clear: I would die and there would be a terrible war among not only our coven, but all supernaturals on this continent. And the only way to bring peace back between all species was if you became the leader. Not only leader of DuMoir Castle, but leader of all vampires."

I gaped at him. "We're at war now."

"I imagined." Lord Reynard let out a long breath. "And you're hiding."

"I don't have much of a choice right now."

"But you intend to fight and reclaim DuMoir Castle?"

"Yes."

"Then I have something that can help you."

My breath caught. "What?"

He touched his chest. "Remember the silver cross I wore around my neck?"

"Yes," I growled. "When I last saw it, Alex was wearing it."

"Find it. Retrieve it," he said. I frowned. "Inside the cross is a red stone. It's called the Blood Amulet, and it carries immense power. If you can find it, if you wear it, and if the amulet accepts you, no vampire will be able to stand up against you. You'll be too powerful, and you'll be able to take control of the throne."

I was guessing Alex was wearing the necklace when I killed him, which meant the Blood Amulet was still on his body, under the ruble of DuMoir Castle.

"I think I know where to find it," I said. "But ... Alex was wearing it when I killed him. He wasn't more powerful than normal."

"Like I said, the amulet has to accept the person who wears it. Only then you'll be able to access its powers."

"The amulet didn't accept Alex," I muttered.

"Because he wasn't worthy," Lord Reynard said. "Just a warning: In order to acquire the amulet, you'll have to make a great sacrifice—a truth you will have to reveal in order to prove you're worthy of the amulet's power."

Right now, I would do anything to end the war as soon as possible and find a way to save Thea. If I got the Blood Amulet, I could cross off one of those items from my to-do list.

"I can't …" Keeran gasped. "Hold it for too much longer."

"I think we're done here," Lord Reynard said. "Goodbye, Drake."

There was so much more I wanted to talk to him about, to ask him, but I couldn't hold him here forever. "Thank you."

"Take the castle back, Drake, and continue my legacy."

Keeran released the power—Lord Reynard became a black shadow before evaporating into the air—and fell on his knees.

"Are you okay?" I hooked an arm around his shoulder and helped him to the couch.

Breathing hard, Keeran lay down. "Give me a minute."

A minute was too long. We had to do something now. "Thomas!" I called out, not so loud as to wake up Thea. Thomas appeared in front of me, his ghost form more transparent than usual. "Is there something wrong?"

Thomas shrugged. "It has been hard to keep my form lately."

"But you can still be around even if we can't see you?"

His brows knotted. "Yes."

"Then I have a favor to ask," I said. "Go to DuMoir Castle and find Alex's body. We were fighting on the staircase leading to the third floor. His body is probably there, under all the stones."

"And?"

"Check to see if he's wearing Lord Reynard's silver cross necklace. I need that."

"That's ominous," he said, sounding every bit like a whiny sixteen-year-old teenager.

"There's a powerful stone hidden inside the amulet. We need it."

"That makes more sense." He saluted me by tapping his hand from his forehead. "I'll get on that."

A moment later, he was gone and I began my favorite hobby: pacing and worrying.

"I'm sorry the spell didn't work," Keeran said, sitting up. "I should have summoned someone who could answer your question, and yet, we summoned Lord Reynard. The only connection that I see here is that he was close to you."

"It's okay," I muttered. "At least we got useful information out of him."

I frowned, thinking of what Lord Reynard had told me. A long time ago, Sarki had had a vision of me being the leader of the vampires. Hell. Each time I thought of myself on the throne, I hated it. I hated that image. I hated what I could turn into once I had all that power in my hands. But ... there was no one else. Not here, not right now. If I didn't take the throne, if I didn't save the vampires and the other supernaturals, things would only spiral out of control more and more. Maybe once everything was orderly again, I could find someone else to rule in my place.

But for a while, I would have to endure it.

And somehow I would make sure Thea lived long enough to see it.

14

THEA

"Are you all gonna stand there and just watch me?"

"Yes," Luana was the first to answer. She was leaning against the open door of the guest bedroom-slash-workshop, her arms crossed, and her eyes narrowed.

I chuckled. "At least one of us is sincere."

Keeran stepped to my side and handed me the vial with white crystal powder. "Here."

I took it from him. "Thank you."

I opened the vial and measured the powder. Then, I mixed it with the other ingredients in the mortar.

"Are you sure it won't take too much energy from you?" Drake asked for the hundredth time. He paced in front of the table, but I decided to ignore him since that was his favorite pastime the last couple of weeks.

Luana groaned. "Ask that one more time and I'll bite you."

Drake glared at her.

"Stop you two," I said, my tone firm. "If you keep bickering, I'm gonna kick you both out of this room."

Keeran snickered. "You know you're talking to a vampire and a werewolf, right?"

I glanced at him. "Which side are you on?"

"If I say yours, what do I get?"

I punched his shoulder, and he had the decency of pretending it hurt.

When I looked at Drake, he was staring at me, a small smile on his lips. Heat spread over my cheeks.

With Keeran's help, and under Drake's and Luana's guarded gazes, I mixed the rest of the ingredients and used a small amount of magic to get the potion going.

I dropped the pestle and stared at the mortar and the thick white liquid inside.

"What now?" Luana asked.

"We should go outside for this next part," I said.

Keeran took the mortar and Drake took my hand. We went to the backyard, where there was a larger lawn area. Per my request, Luana brought two mirrors. One was a mirror the size of my open hand, and the other was the larger mirror from the half bath.

"What do I do with these?" she asked.

"Put them down, side by side, mirror turned to the sky," I explained. She did as I said. "Now, I'll pour the potion over the mirrors, and supposedly, we'll be able to see them."

Drake stepped to my side. "Do you know what you're gonna say to them?"

"I think so," I said, feeling a little intimidated to meet with the witch queens like this. I wasn't requesting their presence. I was demanding it.

They could snap their fingers and break my neck.

I pushed those thoughts and fears aside and focused on what had to be done. We didn't have much choice here.

Taking a deep breath, I poured half of the white potion over one mirror, and the second half over the other.

Next, I lifted my hands over the mirrors and channeled my magic. A small flicker answered and retreated. *Come on*, I begged. I called it again, but only a spark appeared. It started warming my veins, but a second later, it was gone, leaving only cold behind.

I sighed, realizing I might not have the power needed for this spell.

One more time, I focused, calling my magic. I gritted my teeth and implored for it to show up, to hold, to help me. My arms shook.

"Thea ..." Drake's voice was a low growl, a warning.

I ignored him and pushed. If I fainted, so be it. I had to call them.

Then, a big hand landed on my shoulder, and strong, pure magic flooded my veins. I gasped as Keeran lent me his power. Damn, he was strong. But I didn't have time to marvel. Instead, I channeled his magic and called on the witch queens.

A white light shone from the mirror, and a thin veil appeared on top of them—a faint image on the mirror, but instead of reflecting what was in front of it, it showed two figures.

Queen Rosilla of the Bluemoon coven and Queen Sarah of the Blackmarsh coven.

"What is it?" Queen Rosilla asked, her tone harsh.

"Who dared summon me?" Queen Sarah asked, her voice equally cold.

While Queen Sarah looked like the ice queen with her fair skin and long silver braid, Queen Rosilla looked like the summer empress with smooth, black skin and full black curls. And, even at this time of the night, both of them were dressed in full gowns, as if ready for a ball.

Keeran stepped away, so the queens only saw me. "I'm Thea Harrington from the Silverblood coven."

"You!" Queen Sarah hissed. She lifted her hand, showing off the red marks on her skin. "You did this to me."

I pushed aside the exhaustion falling over me and faced them, head held high. "I apologize for that, though I won't lie when I say I wouldn't have done differently if I had the chance."

She clicked her tongue. "What do you want?"

"I want to propose an alliance," I said.

Queen Rosilla laughed. "What? Is that some kind of joke?"

"I don't know how much you know—"

"I know enough," Queen Sarah cut me off. "I heard how you betrayed your coven, hid the heart without telling anyone, and then turned against Princess Morda, saying you're the Witch Queen."

"I heard the same," Queen Rosilla said. "And now you're hiding, afraid of Princess Morda's wrath."

"Do you know what Princess Morda calls herself these days?"

Queen Sarah's fair cheeks turned red. "Queen of All Witches. What a joke. Don't try to tell me she's right."

"She's delusional," Queen Rosilla said.

"She is delusional, and I can prove it," I said.

Queen Sarah narrowed her eyes at me. "What do you mean?"

"I'm not the witch queen as I first thought." I rested my hand on my belly, a gesture that was become a habit. "My daughter is."

"W-what?" Queen Rosilla barked. "What nonsense is this?"

"I'm pregnant, and recently I learned my daughter is not only the witch queen of the Silverblood coven, but she's also Queen of All Witches."

Queen Sarah gaped at me. "That's absurd. There hasn't been a Queen of All Witches in centuries. Over a millennium, actually."

"And you're saying your daughter is the next one." Queen Rosilla scoffed. "How would you know?"

"Because Bagatha told me."

Both queens turned pale.

"W-what?" Queen Rosilla asked.

"But ... we assumed Bagatha died long ago," Queen Sarah said.

"Well, until a while ago, I assumed the Queen of All Witches was a fictitious title used in stories to scare little witches. But turns out, she's real and still alive and powerful."

Queen Sarah's eyes tuned hard. "If she's so powerful, then she should come out of hiding and defeat Morda."

I shook my head. "She's powerful, but not that powerful anymore. Her magic is fading now that a new queen is about to come to life."

Queen Rosilla crossed her arms. "You said you would prove what Morda is saying is a lie, but what you're telling us now may very well be a lie, too."

Queen Sarah's eyes widened. "That's right. Who says you're not lying now?"

"I'm not lying," I insisted.

"That's not convincing anyone," Queen Sarah said.

What could I do to prove to them my words were true? I couldn't show them that Bagatha was alive. Even showing them my growing belly wasn't enough, because this could be a normal witch pregnancy. There was no way to show them the Immortal Vow.

I frowned, worried I wouldn't gain their trust, or even a minute more of their time.

A force burst inside me.

I gasped with its strength. The force, the pure magic, filled my veins and moved my body by itself. My arms extended in front of me and white light shone from my palms. In sync, the queens' eyes turned white. They stood frozen, while the magic acted—a magic coming from my daughter.

After a minute, the light faded and the power retreated.

I opened my mouth to ask them if they were okay, to ask them what exactly had happened, but Queen Sarah put a hand over her heart and said, "I can't explain what that was other than a strong, pure magic. It poured over me and I felt it. I felt her. I felt the Queen of All Witches."

"Me too," Queen Rosilla said, her voice a thin whisper. "I couldn't see her, I couldn't grasp the magic, but I felt her as well. I now believe you're carrying the Queen of All Witches."

Hope bloomed in my chest. "Will you help us now?"

The queens took a moment, thinking.

"I propose we put our differences aside and come together in two full moons to see if we can really work together," Queen Sarah said.

Two full moons. That was almost two months away. By then, I would be on the sixth month of pregnancy. From what we knew, I would be weak and hurting all over.

"Why not earlier?" I asked, hoping I didn't sound that desperate.

"Because this can't be taken lightly," Queen Sarah

explained. "And I would rather have some time to think and talk to my advisors."

"Agreed." Queen Rosilla nodded. "Even if you have us convinced, if we don't do this the right away, we can arouse a rebellion inside our own covens, and that's what we least need right now."

I understood their points, but they didn't understand mine. I wouldn't waste my time explaining to them that my pregnancy would be even worse than a normal witch pregnancy because of the Immortal Vow. I was already grateful they were willing to meet us and try to work together. I would take whatever I could.

"Where do you suggest we meet?" I asked.

"The Undying Well," Queen Rosilla said.

"A sacred placed where our magic was first wrought to earth," Queen Sarah muttered. "No witch can be killed on sacred ground, which makes the Undying Well the perfect place for our meeting."

I nodded. "See you on the second full moon."

15

DRAKE

LIKE THIS, SLEEPING PEACEFULLY IN OUR BED, THEA SEEMED like a normal, beautiful pregnant woman. I could pretend she didn't suffer with pain and exhaustion when she was awake. I could pretend she didn't drink tonic after tonic: one to keep her strength, one to help with the pain, one to make her sleep better, and so on. I could pretend she would be all right in the end.

All of that was far from the freaking truth.

Since the talk with the witches almost two months ago, Thea had gradually grown weaker. She barely got out of bed now, and she barely ate. Half of what she ate, she threw up. And half of the time when she was sleeping, she woke up drenched in sweat because of her terrible nightmares.

Nightmares about our daughter—Morda taking her and raising her as her evil minion; Morda killing her in the most painful ways; Thea and I dying in this war and leaving her alone ...

Nothing I did or said put Thea's mind and heart at ease. To be honest, mine weren't either. I had had two more months searching and following clues, and nothing brought me closer to finding a way of saving Thea. I had even visited Bagatha a couple of times—she was also searching and researching, but to no avail.

If she didn't know how to save Thea, how would I?

But I couldn't give up yet. We still had three months until our daughter's birth. It was plenty of time to find a cure, a solution.

Thea moaned and turned to the side. The thin sheet slid down, revealing her big belly. A smile tugged at the corner of my lips. Thea had always been stunning, but now with her round belly and fuller breasts .... I tsked. Hell, I desired and loved her even more.

I groaned as lust traveled south, giving me a hard on. It had been a while since we had last made love, and I didn't think it would happen again anytime soon. If I allowed my thoughts to wander, I realized that without a way of saving her, I would probably never make love to Thea again.

I could live for all eternity, but without her? What was the point?

I shook my head, pushing those thoughts away. I would find a freaking way to save her, even if I had to trade my immortality for it.

But first, I needed a drink.

Feeling defeated, I dragged my feet to the kitchen.

"Hey," Keeran said from one of the stools at the island. He didn't even lift his head from the pile of dusty books in front of him. I was glad to see someone here was as worried about Thea as I was.

"Hey." I walked to the walk-in pantry and grabbed a bottle of wine from the top rack of the wine cooler, and a bottle from the bottom rack. I brought both to the island and offered one to Keeran. "Here." He raised an eyebrow. "It's wine." I lifted the other bottle. "This one is blood."

Keeran took the bottle from me, and using a bottle opener he found in one of the drawers, he opened and poured a glassful for himself. He got another glass and left it beside the bottle. "For Luana when she comes back."

"She went out for a run again?"

He nodded. "Third time today. And when she's not running, she's helping me go through these books." He gestured to the books spread out everywhere. Soon, I would have to change this house's title from private residence to library.

I sighed. Like Keeran and Luana, I had read through all these books twice or three times. Even the books I bought last week. But besides researching ominous books and visiting museums that could contain witch things disguised as things from other cultures, I didn't know what else to do, where else to look.

Once more feeling the weight of my failure on my shoulders, I opened the bottle and poured the blood onto a wine glass. Because of my pent up frustration, I had done more hunting than I needed this last month, so I stored some of the blood for later. It didn't taste the same as the fresh, warm thing oozing out of a deer's vein, but it gave me the same energy and strength.

Without warning, Thomas blinked into existence right in the middle of the kitchen. Lost in my thoughts, I wasn't ready. My fangs elongated, and I bent my knees to attack.

"Whoa, whoa." Thomas held up his hands. "It's just me."

I retreated my fangs and rolled out my shoulders. "Sorry. My head was somewhere else."

"I know where it was," Thomas said. "I don't have news about that, but I have something else."

My body tensed. "What is it?"

"I finally found Alex's body," he said. "It wasn't in the castle's rubble. The witches moved all the bodies to a mass grave in the forest behind the castle."

"It took you two months to find it?" I snapped. He winced. "Sorry. Sorry. I'm not in a good place right now."

"It's okay," he said, sounding disappointed. "I understand. I was frustrated, too. But I think the witches put some sort of spell around the castle that prevents ghosts from coming inside? I don't know what it is, but I feel like I'm gonna be ripped into smoke and disintegrate whenever I go near the castle. That's why it took me so long to find out the bodies had been moved. Then, I had to find out where they had been buried."

I held his gaze. "I'm thankful for your help."

He shrugged. "It's nothing."

Keeran looked up at me. "What's the plan?"

I bit the inside of my cheek. "I think I'm going to this mass grave."

Keeran stood. "I'm going with you."

"Me too," Thomas said.

I glanced to the stairs and listened. From her slow, steady breathing and heartbeat, Thea was still sleeping. And Luana was still out. Until she came back, I wouldn't feel comfortable leaving Thea alone.

So, I went after her. I tracked Luana's scent and later heard her rapid breathing as she ran through the woods. She sensed me approaching and stopped. In her wolf form, she turned to me.

"I'm going out with Keeran and Thomas," I said. "Can you stay at the house with Thea until we come back?"

She nodded her head once, then ran toward the house. And I met Keeran and Thomas on the way. Keeran thought about trying teleporting again, but since he was out for days last time he did that, he used magic to increase his speed. Still, he wasn't as fast as a vampire, and it took us hours to arrive at the mass grave Thomas had found.

In the dark, I could see the shapes of the trees and a small hill in a clearing. But once Keeran illuminated the place with a red flame on his palm, I could see the hill was moved dirt. This large mount was the mass grave.

And we were now about to dig it up to find Alex's body.

Hell.

Keeran slapped his hands and the flame blinked out, then reappeared in several spots around the clearing, illuminating the mass grave. He stared at the dirt in front of us. "I can try to locate Alex's body, but I'm not sure how it'll go."

Accordingly to Thea, Keeran was powerful, but he still lacked training. Most of the time, he didn't know the spell he could perform. In the past few months, Thea had been trying to teach him all she could, but since she wasn't able to show him anything other than telling him the theory, his training was lacking. Still, he often surprised us with his abilities.

"I wouldn't mind if you wanted to try," I said, hopeful. That would save time and strength.

"By any chance, you don't have anything from him?"

I thought for a minute, but I had never wanted anything Alex had, and I hadn't taken anything from the castle when we fled. "No."

"I can try go to the castle and search his chambers," Thomas said.

"Didn't you say you were having issues getting into the castle?" I asked. "Besides, would you be able to grab whatever you found?" I asked.

Thomas's face fell. "Not for long."

"Then I would have to sneak in there. That would take a long time."

"Not to mention too risky," Keeran said. "It's unlikely you can sneak in a half-destroyed castle full of witches and were-wolves. Besides, who says this Alex's chambers are intact? Maybe a witch moved in and his things were gone."

Hell. "Then you just try the spell however you can perform it. If you find him or not, we begin digging soon."

As expected, the spell didn't work. Under closed eyes and gritted teeth, Keeran searched and searched. There were moments when he thought he was nearing Alex's body, but then the energy snapped and he lost it again.

Meanwhile, we were wasting time.

Before Keeran gave up on the spell, I was already digging.

Two hours later, I was chest deep in turned dirt and lost limbs. The dirt and the dead didn't bother me much when compared to the smell. With my enhanced senses, the rotten smell of decomposing flesh revolved my stomach every two seconds.

Keeran joined me, and he had to run away from the site twice to throw up. I guessed he wasn't used to seeing so many bodies—and touching them.

Meanwhile, Thomas hovered over the site, trying to get glimpses of the bodies emerging from the ground in case we missed something.

Every corpse I found, I pulled out, so I could make sure it wasn't who I was looking for. Most of the bodies here had already started decomposing, and the faces were deformed or half-missing. I hoped I could recognize Alex.

I lost count when I moved fifty bodies and nothing. We kept going, but the hope that we would find Alex here was slowly fading.

Sighing, I stepped back—and tripped on a corpse. I bent down to pull the body out of my way. The back was turned to me, and all I could see was blood and dirt over the messy, brown hair and the white shirt. The moment I grabbed the shoulders, I knew. My eyes widened, and I suddenly could make out his mangled body—his hair, his wide shoulder.

"Here," I shouted as I jumped out of the hole, with the body in my arms. I laid the body on the ground and turned it around.

I sucked in a sharp breath. It was Alex all right, but he had hundreds of open, festered wounds, and dirt in his mouth. I closed my eyes for a moment, disgusted by this scene. One thing was to touch and move the body of a person I didn't know. Not that it was all right, but it was easier. Even though I hadn't liked him and we didn't get along, I hadn't wished such a terrible fate for him. Yes, I had killed the vampire, but if I had a choice, he would have received a proper burial.

Like every dead person here. I didn't care if they were my enemies and had tried to kill me. No one deserved to be thrown in a ditch and left to rot.

If I ever regained control of DuMoir Castle, I would arrange for a proper burial for all the dead in here. That was a promise.

"Where's the amulet?" Thomas asked and my mind returned to the task at hand.

I knelt beside the body and opened his ripped shirt. And

there it was. Lord Reynard's thick, silver cross, lying on his chest as if it had been waiting for me.

I reached out, wrapped my fingers around it, tugged ... and it didn't come off. I tugged again, with more force, but the necklace and the pendant didn't move half an inch.

"What the hell?" I asked, trying it again.

"What's happening?" Thomas asked. "Why can't you take it?"

Keeran knelt on the other side of the body. "Remember what Lord Reynard said. To retrieve the amulet, you'll have to make a great sacrifice."

My inside went cold. "Yes. He said I would have to reveal a truth." At the moment, when Lord Reynard had told me that, I hadn't connected the dots. I thought the truth would be to apologize to Alex's dead body for having killed him. Something like that.

But now that we were here and the necklace wasn't moving, I realized what I had to do. What I had to say.

I looked at Thomas.

"What is it?" he asked. So innocent. So lost. And it was all because of me.

I opened my mouth, but the words caught in my dry throat.

"Drake?" Keeran asked. "What's the problem?"

I didn't take my eyes from the boy I had raised. He had to know the truth. He had to hear it from me. Not only because revealing this sad truth would give me the Blood Amulet, but because he needed it to be set free. He needed to hear it to find peace.

I stuffed my chest and blurted it out, "I was the one who killed your parents."

Thomas's eyes bulged. "But ... but you saved me."

I shook my head. "It was one of the few times I was lost in bloodlust. I couldn't control myself. I had no idea what I was doing. Until you hugged my leg. You were so little for an eight-year-old boy, and you were so scared. You hadn't even seen what I had done to your parents. But the moment you laid your little hands on my leg, I woke up from the daze. I can't even begin to explain how shameful and guilty I felt." He would never know how it hurt me. In the beginning, I could barely look at him without hurting. "But I knew what I could do to try to find forgiveness. I snatched you before Prince Dorian and Albert could find you and made you my blood slave. Though, I never considered you that. To me, you were always my little brother."

Thomas just stared at me, frozen in the air.

"Thomas?" Keeran asked, voice low. "Are you okay?"

Thomas's brows slammed down. "Okay? Am I okay? I just found out I was raised by the monster who killed my parents." He gasped. "The monster who got *me* killed."

I stood. "Thomas, that's not—"

"Shut up!" he shouted. "I hate you. No, hate isn't a strong enough word for what I'm feeling right now." He clenched his fists. "I never want to see you again, in this life or the next."

Just like that, Thomas disappeared.

I stared at the spot where he had stood for some time, but that wouldn't bring him back. He had vanished from sight, but now that he knew the truth behind his parents' death, he would be able to move on to the next world.

A long breath escaped through my gritted teeth and I knelt down beside Alex's body.

"I'm sorry," Keeran said.

"Not more than I am," I whispered.

"What are you gonna do now?"

What was I going to do about Thomas? I had no idea. As far as I knew, he was already gone from this world. Besides feeling incredibly sad about losing him forever, and the festering guilt and shame that would certainly never leave me, I was relieved to have finally told him the truth.

I hoped he really found peace now.

Miserable, I reached for the necklace, and this time when I closed my hand around and pulled, it came easily. "I'm gonna take this home and get ready for a war."

I felt a deep tug inside my chest a few seconds before Drake walked into our bedroom. I stared at him for a moment, a little stunned at seeing him covered in dark blood and dirt. But more than that, what alarmed me was his drooped shoulders and the bleakness in his green eyes.

I stood from the armchair I had been reading in and approached him. "What happened?"

He didn't say anything, and I didn't ask again. Instead, I embraced him and held him tight. He pressed his face to my neck and inhaled deeply. If I wasn't so weak, I would have offered him some of my blood. That was sure to cheer him up.

I didn't know how long we stayed there, embracing each other as if it was the end of the world, but suddenly Drake finally said, "I told Thomas that I killed his parents."

I held him ever tighter. "I'm sorry."

"Me too," he whispered.

He then told me what happened in the last few hours they had been gone. I was glad he had found the Blood

Amulet, but my heart ached for him now that Thomas had left.

"Come on," I said, sliding my hand into his. "I'll prepare a bath for you."

I wished I could have comforted him in another way, but making love was off limits nowadays. Instead, I prepared him a nice, warm bath, and massaged the tension from his shoulders and back.

It was the middle of the night, when we usually stayed up, but this time, Drake went back to bed with me, where he held me tight until we fell asleep.

———

I LOOKED OUT THE WINDOW TO THE FULL MOON RISING ON THE horizon.

"It's time," I said, taking my jacket from the armchair in the corner of the bedroom.

Drake helped me with my jacket. "Are you sure you're okay to go? We can postpone it. No, I can go and you stay."

Since coming back with the amulet three days ago, and losing Thomas, Drake had been unusually quiet and even more protective than before. If it depended on him, I would never leave our bed, let alone our bedroom.

I cupped his face. "I'm fine." It was the truth. Since learning about the pregnancy, I had been weaker and weaker. I didn't think I had ever felt as energetic and healthy as before getting pregnant, but there were a few occasions when I felt well enough to go down to the kitchen and have a meal with the others. Or sit in the living room and read a book. Besides, I had prepared for this moment, by conserving my energy and eating right and drinking lots of Bagatha's tonic.

However, as it went, my well phases never lasted long, so the sooner we left, the faster we would get there before I started feeling too weak again. "I'm ready."

He turned his face toward my hand and placed a soft kiss on my palm. "I love you."

A smile turned my lips up. "To what do I owe this declaration?"

"Nothing. Everything. I just wanted you to know. I love you."

I rose to my tiptoes. "I love you too." I pressed my lips to his, wishing he could really feel my love through my gentle kiss.

Drake's body tensed. His arms wound around my waist, and I sensed the battle in him—the battle for control. The same battle he had been fighting the last couple of months. It hurt me that I couldn't help much with it.

I broke the kiss before it deepened too much, and I lost all the little strength I still had to other things. A great way, but not one I should engage in right now.

Drake rested his forehead on mine and inhaled deeply. "Let's go."

We found Luana and Keeran in the living room, waiting for us. Luana with her leather pants and tunic and braided hair, Keeran in his black clothes and long leather jacket—both looked ready for battle.

Luana held up a small thermal bottle. "I've got more tonic here, just in case."

"Good thinking," Drake said. "Ready?"

The three of us said yes, and a minute later, we marched outside.

Luana glanced up at the full moon. "Um. There are some clouds approaching. I might have to stick to the shadows of the trees, otherwise I won't be able to control my shapeshifting."

She then turned around, took off her clothes, and transformed into her wolf self. Keeran picked up her clothes, folded them, and put them inside a small pouch hanging from his waist.

Luana let out a short howl, indicating she was ready. Together, we trekked to the Undying Well. It was far from the house, so to help out, Keeran put a spell on the both of us to increase our speed. We wouldn't match a vampire and a werewolf, but at least this way we were faster than humans—and I was less tired.

Halfway to the agreed meeting place, Luana slowed down and stopped. We halted beside her as she transformed back into her human body. Avoiding looking at her, Keeran took off his jacket and placed it around her shoulders.

"I smell it too," Drake said.

I glanced around. "What?"

"Blood," Luana said. She held Keeran's jacket tight around her body.

"Where?" Keeran asked.

"This way." Like a cat on the hunt, Drake moved with silent and fast precision. In the blink of an eye, he was leaning over a bush twenty feet away. He let out a deep growl.

We rushed to his side and stared to whatever had ticked him.

My blood chilled.

Weeping, she was crouched beside the trunk of an arching tree, with her dress in rags, and bloody wounds on her legs and hands.

"Ebby," I whispered, not believing the sight in front of me.

"Help," she croaked.

"I'll show you," Drake muttered before advancing on her. I put out my arm just in time and stopped him. "She betrayed you. She deserves to die."

Nobody deserved to die, but Ebby came pretty close. I might be able to convince Drake to not kill her, to leave her, but first, I wanted to know what was going on.

I rested my hand on Drake's chest. "Give me a moment with her," I whispered before kneeling beside her. "What happened?"

Ebby's crying intensified, but she wiped her tears, smearing blood from her hands on her cheeks. "Princess Morda. She tried to kill me."

"Why?"

"Because I failed her again." She sniffed. "I had the opportunity to kill you and lost you. She said she wouldn't tolerate any more mistakes."

I frowned. "How are you alive?"

She stared at me, confused. "What?"

"If Morda wanted to kill you, she would have. How are you alive?"

"Your servant escaped an entire mansion full of witches, why can't I?" she snapped, gesturing to Keeran.

"Because I helped him escape," I said. Her eyes bugged. "Besides, Keeran is stronger than you are."

She wrinkled her nose. "Okay, I confess, it wasn't like that. Like you said, I'm weak." A new tear rolled down her cheek. "Princess Morda called a few witches to her new throne room, me included. At first, I thought it was to assign us a new mission, but when we got there, we learned we would be publicly executed to show the other witches, and the werewolves living in the castle, what happened to people who failed her orders." Her jaw trembled. "She tied us down and started performing the Bloodbone Ritual on us, one by one. Polina was beside me and she panicked. Like your pet had done, Polina used her magic to break free and try to escape. Then chaos ensued. Many other witches got free and fought back. I did too." She held her head high. "In that moment, Princess Morda lost control of the castle and I used that chance to escape."

I pressed my lips together. Publicly killing the witches who had failed her? It did sound like something Morda would do. However, I still found it hard to believe Ebby had escaped.

"Where are the other witches who escaped?"

"I don't know. I didn't pay attention to anything other than running and fleeing." She shrugged. "Maybe they were caught? Maybe a few made it out and are hiding, like me? I don't know!" A sob shook her body.

I glanced to Drake, Luana, and Keeran.

"You can't possibly believe her," Drake said, his eyes hard.

"I'll never believe her again, not completely at least." I stood. "But I can't just leave her here like this."

Drake's jaw ticked. "I love that you're caring and want to help everyone, but some people simply don't deserve your help. And this girl is one of them."

"I understand, but I still can't leave her here."

"Thea, this is insane," Keeran said, his voice tight. Ebby had pretended to be his friend too, and then she turned on both of us. "I get it that you don't want to kill her, but let's just leave her here."

"Leave her here and let's go, or we'll be late," Luana said.

I stepped closer to the group. "Even if she's lying to us, I think we can use her to our advantage. We can pretend to trust her, or let her know we trust her with reservations.

She'll try to prove herself by providing us information about Morda and DuMoir Castle."

"It could be lies," Drake said.

"I know, but maybe her information will be half-lies," I said. "We can catch her with a truth spell or something." I glanced at Keeran. It was a hard spell with rare ingredients, but I thought he was strong enough to do it.

"You're suggesting we take her to the meeting?" Keeran asked. "That's too risky."

"I know, but then she'll see we're not kidding. If she tricks us in any way, she's dead. Besides, meeting the other witches might scare her to the point where she doesn't lie to us."

"I don't like this," Luana said.

"Me neither, but for once, I want to be ahead of Morda," I said. "For once, I want to beat her at her own game. If she sent Ebby here to trick us, then let's pretend we were tricked, and then use her to trick Morda instead."

Keeran frowned. "That makes sense, actually."

Drake shook his head. "I'm against it."

"I still don't like it," Luana said. "But I think it's worth a try."

I stared at Drake. "Please?"

He groaned. It was his away of reluctantly agreeing. I smiled at him for a quick second, before turning to Ebby with a serious expression. "After all you've done to us, we should kill you, or leave you here to rot alone. But that's exactly what we're trying to change in this world. We want more compassion and peace, so we're taking you with us, but know this: You'll have to prove yourself to us."

Ebby wiped her eyes again. "You can trust me, I swear." I extended my hand to her. Eager, Ebby took my hand and I helped her up. "I'll prove to you all I'm telling the truth."

That was fine with me, but for now, we had to keep going. "Keeran, can you heal her wounds a little bit so we can continue?"

Without a word, Keeran knelt in front of Ebby. He hovered his hands over her legs, closing the worst of the wounds and healing her enough so she could walk with us. Then, he stood and did the same with her hands.

"Thank you," she whispered, looking up at him.

Keeran didn't reply and Luana let out a low growl.

"We're wasting time," Drake snapped. "Let's go."

Like he had done before, Keeran spelled the both of us and Ebby so we could run almost as fast as Drake and Luana. After disappearing behind a bush, Luana threw the leather jacket back to Keeran and shifted back to her wolf skin.

And we ran.

But even with the spell, I was starting to feel the ache in my bones, the tiredness in my muscles. I tried to control my breathing and heartbeat as much as I could, because I knew the moment Drake or Luana could hear how tired I was, this trip would be over.

Almost an hour later, we slowed down. Luana appeared by our side in her human body and with the clothes Keeran had brought.

"I can feel it," Keeran said, frowning. "We're near."

"Yes," I said. Even in my state, I also felt the magic pulsing toward us, stronger and stronger each step we took. "We're almost there."

Drake took my hand and gave me the thermal bottle. "Drink."

Of course he knew I was fighting against the pain and exhaustion. With his senses, how wouldn't he? "Thank you." I took the bottle and drank several gulps. To be honest, the tonic only helped a little these days, but every little bit counted.

Still tense, Drake turned to Keeran and Luana, who flanked Ebby. "You two stay back with this one. Keep your eye on her. If she tries anything, kill her."

Ebby's face paled.

I opened my mouth to tell him he didn't need to scare her so much, not yet, but with fast, jerky movements, Drake grabbed my hand and pulled me toward the meeting place.

The closer we got, the stronger the magic was.

"Can you feel it?" I asked Drake. Since he was a vampire, I wasn't sure he felt the same as a witch or a warlock would.

"A little. I feel more tension in the air than magic." He squeezed my hand. "Sorry for being in a bad mood."

I squeezed his hand back. "I understand. And I appreciate you trusting me."

Drake gave a long side glance with those brilliant green eyes. I smiled at him. Damn, he was so handsome. Sometimes I forgot how lucky I was.

I placed my other hand on my belly. Even if I wasn't here to see her grow, our daughter was lucky because she had an awesome father who would take good care of her.

The trees cleared into a tall rock formation with a large opening like a cave.

"The Undying Well is inside?" Drake asked, skeptical.

I shrugged. "It must be. I've never been to this place, but I've heard lots about it."

Supposedly, the magic that witches now possessed had come from the well hidden in here. The well per se didn't possess magic to give anymore, but the ground was a sacred place, and no harm could come to a witch while she was in here.

Drake and I entered the narrow and dark tunnel of the cave. It went on for a couple of minutes, then it started widening until finally it opened to a huge cavern. I halted at the edge of the stone stairs carved out of the rock and gaped at the sacred place—and the many witches waiting for us.

The stairs led to a stream of bright white water that spread like a long snake throughout the place. It sometimes disappeared under the stone walls. In the center of the room, the stream widened, creating a pool where a round stone well rose from the middle of the water. Dormant magic pulsed from inside the stone well.

Around the center pool and well stood Queen Rosilla, Queen Sarah, and a dozen of other witches—their inner circles.

"Thea Harrington," Queen Rosilla said, her loud voice echoing through the cavern.

With Drake by my side, I approached the queens. Like I was taught to do, I bowed my head. "Hello, Queen Rosilla, Queen Sarah. Thank you for coming."

Hiding her burnt hand behind her, Queen Sarah wrinkled her nose at me. Then, she shifted her gaze to Drake. "Who is this?"

Drake also bowed his head to the queens. "I'm Drake, former prince of DuMoir Castle."

"A vampire?" Rosilla asked, frowning.

"A vampire is the father of the Queen of All Witches?" Sarah asked, her tone dubious. Untrusting.

"Yes, Drake is the father of the Queen of All Witches." I rested my hand on my belly. "I see you have talked to your council." I gestured to the witches behind the queens.

Queen Rosilla nodded. "I have and I must say, my coven

isn't happy about uniting with another coven, but I convinced them it was our only choice."

"Good," I said. "And you, Queen Sarah?"

"I've also talked to them." The tightness of her tone didn't bode well.

"And?"

"They want proof."

My brows curled down. "I thought I had proven to you when we first talked. You know I'm carrying the Queen of All Witches."

"I do," Queen Sarah said. "But they want to know it too. To feel it."

What kind of queen was she? Couldn't she order them to believe her, and they had to do it? But if she was that cruel and uncaring, then we were back to square one. We needed leaders, but we needed good leaders, who heard their people and improved their lives.

Karyn, Queen Sarah's second, stepped closer. "You have to understand, most of us never thought the Queen of All Witches was a real thing." I knew what she meant. "As much as we respect and obey Queen Sarah, our queen knows how important it is for us to have proof of such declaration."

Another witch approached us. If I remembered correctly, her name was Tallie and she was part of Queen Sarah's council. "This is a huge moment for us. We would like proof."

I dropped Drake's hand and also placed it on my bump. I closed my eyes and focused—not in calling my magic, but talking to my daughter.

Emotion choked me when I realized I had never really talked to her, not directly. I talked about her, I mentioned her all the time, but despite the fact she was right here with me, I hadn't talked to her.

Hi, baby, I thought. *How is it going in there? I hope you're okay. I'm sorry I'm weak and tired all the time. I'm trying to keep up my strength for your sake, but I can't seem to hold on for long lately. Please, hang in there. Your father and I love you, and you'll make sure you're okay, all right?* My eyes misted. *But I have a request right now. Can you show your power to these witches, please? We need their help, and if we don't prove your destiny to them, they won't help us.*

As if she had been waiting for this moment, my daughter acted. Power exploded from me, pushing everyone back, including Drake. Like it had happened before, the witches' eyes glowed blue as my daughter poured her magic into them.

Then they blinked, but the awe didn't leave their expression.

"Incredible," one witch said.

"It's true," another whispered.

"This is amazing," a third one muttered.

Queen Rosilla smiled. "This is the second time I felt that, and I can honestly say that it was as powerful and emotional as the first time."

"That's one hell of a Queen of All Witches," Queen Sarah said with a smirk.

Thank you, baby.

"I'm glad you're satisfied," I said. Even though it hadn't been my magic, I suddenly felt drained. Black dots appeared at the corner of my vision. Sensing me, Drake pulled me closer so I could discretely lean on him. "Are you going to help us?"

Queen Sarah and Queen Rosilla exchanged a look. Then, they said in unison, "Yes."

Relief course through me.

"But on one condition," Queen Sarah said.

My stomach dropped. What now? She would ask for a sacrifice, for gold, for what? Dread filled my chest. "What is it?"

"We launch an attack on the next full moon," she said.

That was it? I mean, it wasn't the ideal time as I would probably be even weaker by then, but it could have been worse. At least that should be enough time for us to prepare and interrogate Ebby to find out which of her lies would be useful or not.

"What do you think?" I asked Drake.

He nodded. "I'm okay with that."

"Then it's settled," I said. "Next full moon we take Morda down."

I ROLLED FROM THE LEFT TO THE RIGHT, TRYING TO FIND A position that didn't hurt, but now, at seven and a half months, everything hurt. It hurt even when I didn't move. It hurt when I breathed.

But in a couple of hours, everyone was leaving for the final battle, and I had to endure it. I had to because I wanted to go, too. I wanted to squeeze Morda's neck with my own hands.

I sat up, determined to go, but a stab of pain cut down my back and I swallowed a cry.

"Lie back down." Drake rested his hands on my shoulders and pushed me down on the mattress.

"I need to get up." I rose on my elbows and looked at him. "I need to get ready."

His jaw ticked. "We already talked about this, Thea. You can't go."

"I have to!" I snapped. "This is my fight too."

"My love," he said with an exhale. "I know it's your fight too, but I promise you, I'll fight for me, for you, and for our daughter." He leaned over me and kissed my forehead. "In the last month, you've barely been able to get up. I don't think you can do it now. Please, just stay down."

"How can you ask me that when you'll be marching to battle soon? Do you really think I can just lie here and relax?"

"Nobody said anything about relaxing, though you should." He rested his hand on my big bump. At the same time that seven months seemed like an eternity, it had gone by too damn fast. Soon this child would be here—and I would die. "Think of her."

"I am thinking of her, and I need to fight for her."

It was pathetic how I had done nothing this past month. Ever since the meeting with Queen Rosilla and Queen Sarah, I had been practically bedridden. I had been a little skeptical when Queen Sarah had offered to take Ebby and interrogate her, but I gave in because I thought my past with Ebby would interfere with it. I wouldn't want to hurt her, because she had been my friend—or at least pretended to be my friend. However, I had made Queen Sarah swear she wouldn't torture Ebby. That was one of the reasons Drake and I were fighting now: to make a better world for all supernaturals. Torture wasn't a part of that world.

Hopefully, Queen Sarah had reformed Ebby by now, and she was now a faithful member of the Blackmarsh coven.

"Thea, please, listen to reason," Drake whispered. "I won't be able to fight if you go. I'll worry about you and we'll all end up hurt."

Like a spoiled child, I pouted. Because there was nothing else I could do. I couldn't stomp away, I couldn't hit him, and I couldn't cast a simple spell to show him I had it in me. I didn't.

In the end, I knew he was right.

I let out a long sigh. "I know, I know. I just feel so useless staying behind."

One corner of Drake's lips curled up. "You, useless?" He leaned over me and brushed his lips on mine. "You're more important than air, Thea. You'll never be useless." I wound my arms around his neck, pulling him to me, but the moment his lips closed around mine, his body stiffened. He pulled back and glanced to the window. The sun was finally setting, which meant it was almost time. "The witches are here."

As if I weighed nothing, Drake lifted me up and took me to the living room downstairs. He sat me in one of the armchairs and placed a throw blanket over my legs. I smiled at him, always touched by how caring he was.

Luana and Keeran were in the kitchen, eating dinner. I turned my nose up at the sour smell coming from their food. Lately, I had to shove food down my throat because even things I had loved before, now tasted sour and bitter.

Luana turned her head to the door. "The witches are here," she said.

I smiled. It must be nice to be able to hear things far away.

Not five minutes later, Drake opened the door to Queen Rosilla, Queen Sarah, their council, and Ebby. They marched in wearing battle clothes—leather gowns and pants, and with their hair tied out of the way. A chill ran down my spine. How I wished I was well enough to join them.

Dressed in similar fashion, Ebby looked around, as if analyzing our house. What? Was she plotting how she would escape our clutches?

Beside me, Drake put a hand on the back of my chair. "Is everything set?"

"Yes," Queen Rosilla said.

"And you?" Queen Sarah asked. "Ready?"

"Yes," Drake said. "I'll be leaving in a minute and will meet you at the castle." Drake had told me he had several parts to put into action for their attack plan. I didn't like it, but that wouldn't change anything. He leaned over me and pressed his lips on mine. "Please, take care of yourself. I'll be back soon." He kissed me again. "I love you."

I held on to his hand. "Please, be careful."

One corner of his lips tugged up. "Always."

Right.

I blinked and then he was gone. My heart stopped for a moment, then sped up in agony. He was gone. He was going to fight in what we hoped was the last battle in this war. Anything could happen. What if he got hurt? What if he didn't come back?

"Deep breaths," Luana said from the kitchen. She probably had picked up my rapid heartbeat and breathing.

I inhaled deeply, then faced Queen Sarah. "Found anything useful?"

Queen Sarah glanced at Ebby before returning her gaze to me. "Not much. Apparently Morda didn't tell her much."

"Or she's hiding it."

"With the methods I used, only if she's an extremely powerful witch," Queen Sarah said.

I cringed thinking of the methods she could have used, but at least Ebby was here, still standing and looking healthy. Whatever it was, it didn't leave a permanent mark. Moreover, Ebby wasn't a powerful witch, so she couldn't have resisted.

Queen Rosilla narrowed her eyes at me. "Are you staying here alone?"

"No, I'm staying with her," Keeran said from the kitchen. Last night, Luana had told me she was torn. She wanted to stay with me, but she also wanted to go and have her revenge on Ulric. I told her to go. I had also told Keeran to go, but he wasn't having it.

The queens turned their noses to him. I knew what they were thinking. A warlock right beside them. They were eager to kill him. I would like to see them try.

Thankfully, it wouldn't come to that.

"I already told you, I would rather you go and make sure Drake and Luana are fine," I told him. He shook his head. "Keeran, don't make me use my magic to force you to go."

He snickered. What? He didn't think I could do it? Truth was, unless my daughter lent me her magic, I probably couldn't.

"I can leave a couple of my witches here to guard you," Queen Sarah offered.

"I-I'll stay," Ebby muttered. She raised her timid eyes to me. "I would like to stay and watch over Thea."

Did she really think I would let her be alone with me?

"By all that's sacred." Queen Sarah tsked. "As if I would trust you with this. You're coming with me so I can keep an eye on you!"

I liked that plan. I sighed, already too exhausted from talking—and worrying. The battle hadn't even begun, and I was already dying of worry.

"I'm fine," I said, my tone firm. "I'll be fine by myself. Nobody knows where this house is, and we need everyone able to fight at the battle. Please, don't worry about me."

Keeran frowned, but didn't say anything else.

Thankfully, the queens didn't push the matter. And soon, they were all marching out of the house.

Keeran and Luana stayed inside as everyone left.

"Are you sure you want me to go?" Keeran asked, his voice tight.

"Yes," I insisted. "Go and make sure this hot-blooded wolf —" I jerked my chin. "—doesn't do anything stupid."

Keeran snorted. "Because that's easy."

Luana gaped at him. "What's that supposed to mean?"

I chuckled. "All right, you two. Out. You need to go." I picked up a book from the end table and pretended to be entertained by the words on the page so I wouldn't cry.

Keeran and Luana left.

I glanced at the living room, dining room, and kitchen. Except for the books cluttering the place, they were all empty now.

All of a sudden, I felt alone.

And worried. Very worried.

This time when I returned my eyes to the book, I really focused on the words. I had to find some distraction so I wouldn't go crazy. At least, this was a good book—a contemporary romance about a girl who inherited a ranch from her grandmother and her talent as a horse whisperer.

Hours passed. With difficulty, I got up, made a small snack, drank some of Bagatha's tonic, then went to the couch, where I lay down and ended up napping.

A loud boom woke me up.

Heart racing, I sat up with a jerk—pain ricocheted through my back and lower abdomen. I stared at the broken glass shards of the porch door and the billowing curtain.

The knob turned.

My breath caught.

The broken door slid open.

Morda stepped in.

SINCE THE FALL OF DUMOIR CASTLE, THE SMALL TOWN OF Crimson Glen had been overtaken by vampires—at first by the rebel vampires who didn't want any rules. However, the princes and nobles, tired of hiding in the forest, had moved in too. In no time, the vampires had killed half the town's residents, and enslaved the other half—to feed on later.

The town was a mess, but it was exactly where I had to go.

It was two hours after sunset, and the town was starting to come alive. As I walked down Main Street toward the town's square, I saw as the vampires left their new homes and started partying. They looked drunk as they loitered in the streets. A few of them had blood slaves in their arms. They laughed, they chatted, they snickered—all loudly. It felt like walking into the French Quarter of New Orleans during Mardi Gras: a never-ending party.

But instead of alcohol, the residents here were drunk on blood.

I hadn't walked one block before the vampires noticed me. Besides a few known faces from the castle, most of them were rebel vampires who had lived with Lark and Remi in the village. But even if I didn't know them all, they knew me. They all knew who I was.

The farther I went, the more vampires noticed my presence. They stopped and watched me. Some even followed me, but always keeping their distance.

I saw the town's square. I hadn't been here much, but I knew that once upon a time, the train that took humans to visit DuMoir Castle left from the station off the square.

One block from the square, I turned left. Halfway down the block, and with at least a hundred vampires tailing me, I halted in the middle of the street, facing a modest townhouse.

The front door opened and Dorian stepped out, his eyes wide. "What are you doing here?"

Aston, Gray, Cain, and Patrick appeared behind him.

"Hello, my brothers," I said.

"We heard rumors you had died," Cain said.

"That Morda had killed you," Patrick added.

"I heard it had been the werewolf alpha," Gray objected.

I smiled. "As you can see, I'm alive and well." My smile faded. "Where's Nolan and Phelps?"

"Gone," Patrick said, his tone upset.

"Nolan was killed by a werewolf, and Phelps by a witch," Cain said.

Hell.

"What are you doing here?" Dorian repeated his question.

"I want to know what *you* are doing here." I glanced to my sides, to the vampires forming a wide arc around me. "I thought you were princes. Why are you hiding like this?"

Patrick scoffed. "Have you really been out of the loop, or are you pretending again?"

Again … so they knew I had feigned losing my memory months ago? That was okay. That was in the past.

"I know the castle was taken from us, disgraced by witches and werewolves. I know the princes of DuMoir Castle are hiding among rebel vampires who couldn't care less about them."

Dorian growled. "Do you think we had a choice? We have been roaming in the forest, trying not to succumb to our primitive instincts. We only joined the rebels after they had sacked this town."

"We had no other choice," Cain said.

Behind me, growls echoed.

"I'm attacking DuMoir Castle," I told them. "Tonight. Join me."

"How?" Aston frowned. "How can you win against the witches and werewolves?"

"I've got the allegiance of the Blackmarsh and Bluemoon covens, and I'm hoping to get yours too."

A short vampire with massive arms stepped forward. "When they came into the town, they knew what they were getting into," he said. "They live here, but it's by our rules."

"I thought you guys didn't have rules," I teased.

"We have only one," he said with a snarl. "These vampires —" He jerked his chin toward the princes. "—have no title and are now imprisoned to this town."

What the hell?

"I think you're about to lose your one rule, because not only will they come with me, but you will too."

Short and Stocky laughed. "My vampires won't follow you."

I cocked an eyebrow. "Your vampires?" I quickly found Lewis and Holden in the back, as if afraid of defying the rebels. "I recognize a lot of *my* vampires in the bunch." I beckoned them forward. "Come join us. I'll protect you."

As expected, Lewis and Holden were the firsts to push through the crowd and stand behind me. Another dozen joined us.

Short and Stocky glared at us. "That's only a handful. I can still squash you."

"Once I give my order, you won't be able to," I said. I knew I was pushing his buttons, but it was freaking fun.

"Order?" He spat. "What makes you think we'll obey you?"

"If you don't, I'll make you."

He growled, along with his vampires. "I would like to see you try."

They attacked.

The vampires lunged at me, and the princes appeared by my side to help me.

As stronger princes and trained vampires, my side could fight like this forever. We would eventually win, but this time, we didn't have days. We had to finish this ridiculous fight now.

I felt the magic of the amulet rushing through my veins as I wrapped my fingers around Short and Stocky's throat and threw him to the ground. As a vampire, I had been fast and strong, but now with the power of the amulet, I was on an entirely new level. The vampires didn't even have time to react before I overpowered them.

So that was why Lord Reynard had been so damn powerful. It was a blessing Alex hadn't known how to access the amulet—he probably didn't even know there was an amulet inside Lord Reynard's pendant.

I put down vampire after vampire, until even the princes stepped back and stared at me, their eyes wide.

Finally, the attacks stopped and the vampires hung back, apprehensive.

"You cannot defeat me," I said with a growl. "Now that you've seen what I can do, join me. I'm marching to DuMoir Castle to claim it back right now!"

"Even with your abilities, that's suicide," a vampire said.

"It won't be," I said. "We have two witch covens on our side, and we'll have more allies as soon as we get to the castle." We were wasting time here. "Say you'll join me now."

Ninety percent of the vampires joined me. Most seemed reluctant, but I knew that once they saw our team winning against Morda and her witches, they would understand this was our time. We wouldn't lose.

Lewis stood tall beside me. "Lead us, my prince."

A confident grin spread on my lips. "Let's go to war!"

19

DRAKE

I was late and the witches, greedy as they were, didn't wait for me. They had already invaded the castle and the battle had started.

"Hell," I muttered as I watched the spark of lights flying from the castle's windows.

"What now?" Cain asked.

"Now ... just go in and win this battle," I said. "But be careful with the werewolves. Don't hurt them if you can."

"Why?" Dorian asked.

"I have a plan. Just trust me." I sent them off like a general watching his battalion marching to battle from the top of a hill.

The vampires seemed eager—to either kill or get the castle back, I wasn't sure. Whatever it was, I would deal with that later. Right now, I had another task in the endless plan to accomplish.

Using the power of the Blood Amulet, I focused and listened. I found Luana and Keeran fighting outside the castle, waiting for me. I joined them.

In her wolf form, Luana sensed me coming and howled at me, and by the sound of it, she was mad.

"She wants to know what took you so long," Keeran said.

I raised an eyebrow. "How do you know what she's saying?"

He shrugged. "I just know."

"I had a little bit of a fight," I said, joining them against a group of Silverblood witches.

Keeran cast a powerful shield between us. "I'll distract them with magic. You two approach them and rip them to pieces."

Luana and I nodded.

Keeran dropped the shield and raised his hands toward the witches. A volley of red bolts flew at them—some were a direct hit, some went in a spiral or circles, distracting them.

And Luana and I ran at the witches from the sides. The moment we lunged at them, Keeran stopped his assault. Instead, he ran to us. He grabbed a witch's shoulders and groaned. His hands turned orange, and under his palm, the witch's skin became charred. Keeran slid a hand down, right in the center of her chest. The red light intensified and the orange of his hand grew black. She screamed as Keeran burned her heart from the inside out.

Meanwhile, Luana ripped some throats out, and I ripped out their hearts.

In a matter of seconds, the three of us had defeated over a dozen witches. We formed a good group—we were just missing Thea and Thomas—and we would prove how good we were.

Luana shifted into her human form. Keeran and I kept our eyes on her face.

"I can hear him," she said. "He's in the same room as before, guarding the Silverblood's heart."

"Let's go," I said.

She shifted back into a wolf, and we ran into the castle. We had to fight our way in, but it was mostly witches from the Silverblood, but I wasn't afraid of hurting those.

Five wolves stood at the entrance to the main library room, fighting against a couple of Blackmarsh witches. Inside, Ulric marched side to side, still in his human form.

Hell.

Though I didn't want to hurt many of the wolves, there was no choice here. Keeran and I helped the Blackmarsh witches against the wolves, while Luana sneaked inside.

"My dear wolf," Ulric said, his voice dripping with fake sweetness. "Have you come back to our pack?"

She snarled at him.

With a wicked smile, Ulric transformed into his big brown wolf.

Since I had promised Luana that Ulric was hers, I tried focusing on my fight, but it was hard. Ulric had been alpha for a long time, and he was huge compared to Luana. I couldn't help but pay attention, because if I knew Luana was losing, I wouldn't let Ulric kill her, no matter what. But if I interfered, our plan would go down the drain.

To become alpha of her pack, Luana had to kill Ulric alone.

So Keeran and I stayed by the entrance, keeping out the witches and wolves that came, while Ulric and Luana fought.

The alpha lunged for her, but being small, Luana was more agile. She easily sidestepped him. But Ulric wasn't stupid. Being the alpha, he had probably been challenged a thousand times. He was an experienced fighter. When Luana dodged his attack, he adjusted his feet and turned toward her again. He rammed into her side, sending her sliding back. Luana's paws scratched the floor as she brought herself to a stop.

She limped once, but then she was sprinting, getting out of the way when Ulric rushed for her again. Luana jumped up, springing from a shelf. She arched over Ulric and landed on his back. Fast, she bit down on his shoulder.

Using his brute force, Ulric pushed her against a pillar. Luana let go of him and let out a yelp.

Beside me, Keeran tensed each time she got hit. Apparently, he was also paying attention to her, despite his own fight.

Luana limped away from the pillar. She turned toward Ulric and waited. After showing off for a moment, Ulric came for her. She dodged to the side again, but limping she wasn't fast enough. He closed his jaw around her side. A shrill yelp ripped out of her throat.

Keeran turned toward the fight. I quickly pushed back the wolf I had been fighting, and grabbed his arm. "Not yet," I whispered.

As if to show us she was okay, Luana let out a growl and scratched at Ulric's face, drawing blood. Ulric let her go. Instead of using a few seconds to recover, Luana reacted right away. She bit down on his paw—hard.

Ulric shook her off and limped away, putting some distance between them. From here, I could listen to their accelerated heartbeats and breathing. Though he looked tougher, Ulric was as distressed as Luana, which made me a little more confident she could do this.

Then Ulric charged her again. Luana got out of the way, but Ulric closed his mouth on her paw and threw her at the wall. He came with her and clamped down on her shoulder.

Luana howled.

I stepped forward, ready to kill Ulric myself before he ripped Luana's throat. Keeran put his arm out, stopping me.

"Keep the wolves busy," he said in a low voice.

Understanding what he meant, I turned toward the wolves trying to break through our barrier and fought them. To take on so many by myself, I had to use the power of the Blood Amulet. But it was worth it when I saw Keeran closing his eyes and focusing.

Ulric twisted to the side, as if a jolt of pain had coursed through his body, and he let go of Luana. That was enough to give her an opening. Before Ulric could do anything else, Luana went for his throat.

Blood gushed down her coat.

Three seconds later, Luana stepped back from Ulric's body. Her paws trembled and she collapsed. Keeran put up a strong shield on the entrance before running to her. I quickly finished the Silverblood witch I had been fighting and joined them.

Trembling, Luana shifted back to her human form. I winced at the bloody wounds on her ribs and shoulder. Keeran took off his jacket and covered her naked body.

"You'll be fine," he said, laying his hand on her wounds. He closed his eyes and started healing her. A moment later, Luana's trembling lessened and her breathing slowed. "I didn't heal it that well because we don't have time and it'll take too much of my energy, but it should be enough to hold for now. I'll heal you properly once we're back home, okay?"

She pushed off the floor and Keeran helped her sit up. "Thank you."

"Are you okay?" I asked.

She took in a long breath. "I'll live." Her eyes shifted to the dead wolf on the other side of the room. "For a moment there, I didn't think I would be able to do it."

Hell.

I swallowed, knowing this was another secret I would try taking to my grave. Keeran lowered his head, clearly uncomfortable with the lie.

I cleared my throat. "Are you ready?"

She nodded. "As I'll ever be."

Keeran helped Luana stand. Her skin was pale and her forehead sweaty, but she would be all right. Luana tugged the jacket tighter around her body as she leaned into Keeran for support.

As Keeran tended to Luana, I turned to the pedestal with the heart. I reached for it, but the moment my fingers touched it, the heart exploded in a cloud of smoke. A fake. Of course, Morda wouldn't have left the heart out during a big battle. She probably had the heart on her. That was okay. I would kill her, then get the heart and hand it to Thea.

The three of us exited the room and the wolves at the entrance bowed their heads to her. As we walked down the hallway, we crossed several wolves, and they all stopped and bowed to her. Knowing the alpha was an ingrained trait of the werewolves.

And now, as Luana marched down the hallway, the wolves knew she had defeated Ulric and was now the new alpha of the Dark Vale pack.

We found the foyer, where many more wolves stopped

and showed respect to their alpha. Finally, Luana stopped and turned to them.

"I command you to join the vampires and the Blackmarsh and the Bluemoon covens," she said—loud but not clear. Her voice trembled as if it was too hard to speak. "Attack Morda and her witches!"

The wolves let out a synchronized howl and turned their backs on their current targets. They all ran toward the main dining room.

"That's where Morda must be," I said.

"Go," Keeran said. "Take Morda's heart out. I'll stay behind and take care of Luana."

Luana pushed him away. "I don't need to be taken care of." She swayed to the side.

Keeran wrapped his hand around her elbows and pulled her back to him. "Obviously." He shot me a confident look. "Go."

I nodded once, then ran to the dining room.

There, Morda's right arm Soraya took the show with the inner circle. They stood in a ring in the middle of the room, fighting the werewolves and other witches. Dodging the fights, I approached them.

Morda was nowhere to be seen, but what I didn't expect was too see Ebby kneeling at Soraya's feet, crying a river.

Soraya turned her hand and Ebby shoulders twisted in an awkward, painful way. She screamed.

What the hell was going on?

I pushed through the circle, taking out the witches that came for me without even blinking.

Soraya raised her hand. "Let him come."

The witches stopped attacking me, but hovered close, ready to blast me.

I halted a good six feet from Soraya. "Where's Morda?"

A wicked smile stretched over Soraya's lips. "Isn't that an interesting question? Before I answer that, I have a little tale to tell you."

I growled. "I'm not interested in your tales."

"Oh, but you'll love this one," she said.

The magic of the Blood Amulet rushed through me. I growled again, and this time, the windows shook. "To hell with your tales. Just tell me where Morda is!"

"So impatient." She tsked. "Where do you think she is?"

What?

No.

I stared at Ebby, twisting and screaming on the floor. I had no idea if she had betrayed us or if she was being betrayed, but there was something she could have told Morda.

"It can't be," I whispered.

Soraya raised her chin, and sounding way too eager, she said, "Morda is on her way to Thea right now."

My blood turned to ice. I stared at Ebby, rage consuming my muscles. "I'll kill you."

Soraya turned her hand. Ebby's neck snapped. Her limp body fell to the ground. "Sorry, I've wanted to do that for a long time." I just stared, confused. She went on, "Don't worry. I'll kill you and you'll soon join your beloved, and your daughter, in the afterlife."

I faltered.

They knew about my daughter.

The power inside me built.

Then, a hand clamped down my shoulder.

"Go to Thea," Keeran said, his eyes on Soraya. "I've got this."

Soraya's smile widened. "Oh, hello, lover. I've missed you."

The repulsion in Keeran's stare was enough to convince me he could do this. "Go," he snarled.

I didn't waste another second. I ran out of the castle and through the forest like I had never run before.

20

THEA

I JUMPED TO MY FEET; MY HEART LEAPED OUT OF MY CHEST.

"M-morda," I muttered, not believing my eyes.

"Hello, dear Thea." Dragging her long, black gown across the floor, she walked closer and took a look around. "So this is where you've been hiding? Not too bad."

I stepped back, putting the coffee table between us. "How did you know where to find me?"

"To be honest, it was a surprise, really. A very good one."

"What do you mean?"

She offered me a wicked smile. "It was all because of that wretched Ebby."

"So she did betray us. Again," I whispered.

"Oh yes, dear, but not the way you think."

"What do you mean?"

"After I tried to kill her, I thought I had seen the last of that girl. But to my surprise, when the Blackmarsh and the Bluemoon covens attacked a couple of hours ago, she was with them. And she came straight to me, begging for mercy.

She said that if I allowed her back into the coven, she would tell me where you were."

I gasped. Morda hadn't sent Ebby here. She really had escaped death, but she thought that if she offered something better, Morda would forgive her. Foolish girl.

"Of course, I told her I would welcome her back, and she told me where to find you."

I took another step back. "Where is she now?"

"Being tortured by Soraya."

"But ... she told you where I am."

She brushed at her shoulder as if there had been a speck of dirt there. "She's still a weak and incompetent witch who failed me several times. At least she told me one useful thing before her petty life came to an end." She waved her hand and the coffee table flew away. It exploded against the wall; the glass shard and wood splinters flew across the room. "Now I shall end another life." She looked at my midsection. "Or shall I say two lives?"

The blood drained from my face. I took another step back. "Morda, you are a princess of the Silverblood—"

"I'm a queen!" she yelled. "I'm the freaking Queen of All Witches!"

I shook my head. "Please, Morda, listen to reason. You did everything for our coven. You were a great leader, and you can still be one, but you have to recognize that my daughter is the queen. If you let me, I can show you her power, and you too will believe—"

"She'll never be queen, because she won't be born."

The murderous gleam in her eyes sent a chill up my spine. I shut my mouth and ran. Despite the pain coursing through every one of my muscles, despite the tiredness overcoming my senses, I ran. The bolt Morda had conjured hit the shelf on the wall instead, burning a hole into it.

There was no talking to her. Morda was incapable of hearing, of understanding anything right now. Even if I tied her down and showed her my daughter's power, she would still deny it. She would still fight against it.

But I had no power of my own to fight her, either.

My only option was to run.

So I ran.

I pushed past the pain, past the aches. I bumped into furniture. I tripped over rugs and steps. No matter what I did, I was neither faster nor more powerful than Morda, not now. Not at this stage of my pregnancy.

Trying to get away, I went up the stairs and entered the small library. Morda followed me, always shooting spells at me. I didn't know if it was dumb luck or if there was something else going on, but none hit me. I felt them zooming past my shoulder, my ear, my hair, but other than a scare, the spells didn't get me.

I crossed the library and ran into the adjacent office, then I exited through the main door and locked it. Again, I knew it wouldn't hold Morda, but it would give me the one or two seconds I needed to save my life, to save my daughter's life.

Out in the hallway, I threw my shoe down the hallway, as if I had gone into one of the bedrooms but had tripped on the way, and ran down the stairs again. Three seconds later, the office's door exploded and Morda charged out.

"Where are you, little witch? Don't you know I'll kill you no matter what?"

As long as I still had breath in me, I wouldn't stop trying.

Careful with my movements, I tiptoed across the kitchen

and left through the broken door. The shards of glass dug into my bare feet, but I gritted my teeth and endured.

Out on the porch, I ran again.

I dashed down the front steps and—

Morda jumped in front of me.

I fell on my butt and hit my back on the steps. Tears of pain and desperation filled my eyes.

"Where do you think you're going?" She threw a bolt at me.

I raised my hand and closed my eyes, praying that it was quick.

A sound like sparks made me open my eyes and I gasped. A shield of blue light was between Morda and me.

"By all that is sacred," I whispered, amazed at my daughter's powers. And she hadn't even been born yet.

Morda let out a scream and a stream of magic. The shield trembled, but held. And I pushed the stairs to help me stand up. Pain ricocheted through my back, down my legs, but I gritted my teeth and blinked back tears. I could die of pain later. Right now, I had to ignore it as much as I could and run away.

I dragged myself up the porch steps.

Morda threw a wave of magic.

The shield broke.

In a flash, she was on me, pushing me against the wall, one hand on my throat, the other over my belly.

"I will kill you," she said in a snarl.

She pulled a red mass from inside her gown's pocket—the heart of the first witch of the Silverblood coven.

My eyes widened.

Using the heart's magic, she pushed against my stomach.

I extended my arms and tried pushing her away, but she didn't budge. I was too weak and drained of magic.

A current jolted through me and a faint shield pushed Morda back.

"That won't cut it this time." She threw a big spell against the shield and it broke instantly.

Another shield blinked into existence, but it faded away by itself.

I was tired. My daughter was tired.

We were no match for Morda and the heart.

My legs gave out, and I fell to my knees.

"Oh no, not yet." Morda's magic wrapped against my arms and pulled me up. Her eyes glinting with madness, Morda leaned over me. "Now, I shall kill your daughter. Then, I'll kill you. Very slowly."

She pressed her hand against my belly.

I cried out.

A wind like a hurricane pushed us to the side. When I blinked, Morda was down on the other side of the porch.

And Drake stood between us. "No, Morda. I'm the one who's gonna kill you."

21

DRAKE

THE HOUSE WASN'T CLOSE TO THE CASTLE, BUT RUNNING ACROSS the forest while counting the seconds until I could see Thea with my own eyes and make sure she was okay, the distance seemed infinite.

I was thankful for the power the Blood Amulet gave me. It made me faster than I had ever been before. And I was able to arrive at the house in time to see Morda cornering Thea.

Rage filled my chest and I rushed Morda, sending her flying down the length of the porch—but not before snatching the coven's heart from her hand.

Beside me, Thea slid to the floor. I wrapped my arms around her and kept her up. "Are you okay?" I looked at her, as best as I could, to make sure she wasn't hurt. "Is our daughter okay?"

"I'm fine," she whispered. She was lying. She might not be hurt, but her heartbeat was erratic and she was having trouble breathing.

In no time, Morda was back on her feet and flinging a spell at us. With my speed, I picked up Thea and carried her to the dining room. I placed a chair in a hidden corner and sat her down. I handed her coven's heart to her.

Thea cradled it like it could break at the slightest contact.

"Stay here," I told her, before going back to the porch.

Morda's spell faded in her hand. She blinked. "Where's—?"

I had been so fast, she hadn't seen anything. "I took the heart to the real owner." I smiled. "Your fight is with me now."

She clenched her hands, a black flame enveloping them. "So be it."

When Morda flung the flames at me, I was ready. With my speed, I could deflect all of the bolts she threw at me with ease. My only strategy now was to let her waste her magic and get tired. Then, it would be easy to finish her.

But that could take hours, and I wanted to end this fast.

Dodging her spells, I ran toward her. Before she could realize I was standing right in front of her, I punched her square in the face. A little remorse snaked into my core—I didn't like hitting women, but I tried remembering Morda wasn't a normal woman. She was evil and would do worse to anyone if she had the chance.

With the force of my punch, she flew off the porch. She hit a big tree several feet away from the house and fell to her knees. A blow like that would have killed a human, but Morda, being a powerful princess witch, wiped the blood from her nose, rolled her shoulders, and stood. Her feet were wobbly for two seconds, but then she channeled her magic again.

I ran toward her—the farther we were from the house, the safer Thea would be. As I expected, Morda raised her arms, bringing up a shield between us. Then, she let out her magic—a wave of black light that rippled in all directions. I had nowhere to run, but away.

It took me a second to react and it cost me. The wave of magic hit me in the back, and I fell face-first on the dirty ground. Morda sent out another wave, lower this time, so it wouldn't miss me even if I was lying down. Using my speed, I jumped and ran to the nearest tree. I hid behind it as the magic washed by. The tree groaned in protest as the magic burned its trunk.

Trying to distract her, I broke off some branches, ripped the ends so they were pointy, and threw them at her with precision. But her shield was so damn powerful, my improvised weapons burned to a crisp the moment they touched her magic.

I didn't know what else to do.

My concern only increased when Morda started sending the magic waves farther and farther, trying to hit me. Soon, she would reach the house and hurt Thea. I had to stop her now.

In the second between waves of magic, I sneaked a peek at Morda.

Right then, a white shadow appeared in front of her. Startled, Morda screamed and fell back, losing the hold on her magic. The white shadow took form and Thomas appeared.

I wasted a precious moment gawking at him, but soon ran toward Morda.

Still on the ground, she saw me coming and lifted the shield again. I bumped into it and groaned as little shocks rushed through my body. She sent the magic wave again, and I ran back to the tree.

Thomas blinked into existence in front of me.

"I thought that would help more," he said.

"It's okay." An idea came to me. "Thea is inside the house. Go to her and get her out of here before the magic reaches the house and she gets hurt."

Thomas frowned. "Thea isn't one to take orders from anyone."

"Tell her I'm begging. She'll know I mean it."

After one sharp nod of his head, Thomas disappeared.

Another wave of magic washed past me and the tree shook. Soon, it would snap and fall over my head.

The amulet warmed against my chest. I glanced down at the silver cross hiding it. The heat increased, almost burning me.

A tug cut through me.

The amulet was telling me something.

Following the amulet's call, I walked toward Morda. She grinned at me, probably thinking I was stupid, and sent another wave of magic. I gritted my teeth, expecting it to burn or to send me flying.

But right before the magic reached me, the amulet's power filled my veins. As the magic brushed my skin, little jolts prickled my body. It hurt, but it was bearable. Morda's eyes widened in shock. This time, I grinned at her. I rushed forward and she sent more magic at me. Again, the pain was nothing I couldn't take.

Although, I paused before the shield. I clenched my hands and stepped through. The pain prickling my skin was ten times stronger, but the amulet worked, filling me with more of its power.

"Impossible," Morda whispered, her eyes wider and wider.

"Improbable, not impossible," I said, repeating what

Bagatha had told us before. After all I had seen in my five hundred years, I really believed nothing was impossible.

I bared my fangs and lunged at her.

Morda stepped back and pulled out a dagger from the side of her gown. I had expected her to react with magic, not with a weapon. With the momentum I had invested in my attack, I couldn't pull back fast enough. I was able to stop myself before she pierced my heart, but she swiped the dagger to the side, cutting my chest.

Cutting the necklace's chain.

The amulet fell to the ground.

Its power faded in a second.

With a wicked gleam in her eyes, Morda extended her hand. An invisible force wrapped around my neck and pulled me up and up, until I was hovering a foot from the ground. The force intensified and I gagged.

"Poor little vampire," Morda teased. "Did you really think you could defeat me?"

Power crackled through the air.

"Maybe he can't, but I can."

I fell to the ground on my knees. Blinking and gasping for air, I looked up and found Thea standing by my side— holding her coven's heart in her hand.

Morda's face paled as she jerked her shoulders, trying to get rid of whatever spell Thea had over her.

Her eyes on Morda, Thea extended her hand to me. I took it and stood beside her. She squeezed my hand and I felt it. More power—new power. It came from my core, from my dead heart.

The Immortal Vow.

Thea channeled the power of the Immortal Vow, and together, we immobilized Morda.

I wasn't sure how it worked, but the Immortal Vow guided me. I bent down and grabbed the Blood Amulet, then I stepped forward and pressed it against Morda's chest.

Her eyes widened and a scream ripped from her throat. From underneath the amulet, a black mark appeared. It slowly spread, killing her inch by inch.

Her entire body turned black.

Morda erupted into ashes.

A breeze rolled by, carrying her away.

I squeezed Thea's hand. "We made it." I smiled at her.

Thea blinked, as if waking from a daze, then she collapsed into my arms.

22

THEA

DRAKE'S FACE WAS TERRIBLY PALE AS HE CARRIED ME INSIDE THE house and laid me on the couch.

"Are you okay?" he asked, his voice trembling. He ran a hand over my forehead, down my messy hair. "Thea, talk to me."

Thomas appeared behind Drake. "I think she's too weak to talk."

Drake snapped his head to Thomas. "I thought I told you to take her away."

"I tried, but she wasn't having it." He looked down at his hands. "It isn't like I can grab her and drag her off."

Drake ran a hand through his hair, then leaned over me. "I know you're not okay. Tell me what it is so I can help you."

"I'm f-fine," I lied, my voice barely a whisper. The last bit of magic had drained me completely. I knew most of the power had been borrowed from our daughter, but it had still coursed through me and taken my energy. Pain pinched every inch of my body, but I was too numb and tired to cry. "I'll be fine."

"The hell you will," Drake barked. Tears filled his eyes. "There has to be something I can do." He rested his hand on my belly. A second later, our daughter kicked, right at his hand. His eyes widened. "Did you feel that?"

I offered him a small smile. I had no idea it was so great to watch him this excited about our kid. "I did. I think she wants to give you a high five."

He placed his other hand on my stomach. "I'm here, sweetie." As if she knew exactly where he was touching, our daughter kicked again, directly under his palms. Drake smiled.

Power bloomed inside me. Feeling it, Drake sucked in a sharp breath. It was slow at first, but it spread quickly. While the power he had used to defeat Morda had rushed through me and out of me and taken some of my magic with it, it was different this time. This magic warmed my core and soothed me from the inside out. My muscles relaxed, the pain faded, the dizziness disappeared. I closed my eyes for a moment and breathed deeply, letting it all refresh me.

When I opened my eyes again, I felt better than I had in months. I wasn't pain free, or exhaustion free, but at least I could move on my own without being afraid of collapsing in half a second.

"What happened?" Thomas asked. He and Drake had a similar expression: round eyes, slack jaw, and tight shoulders.

I sat up and looked down at my body. "I think she gave me some of her magic."

Drake kissed my belly. "Thank you," he whispered, putting another smile on my lips.

Then I saw the blood smeared on his ripped shirt. "You're hurt." I reached for him.

Drake opened his shirt and showed his wound to me. "It wasn't deep and it's already healing."

"But we can still apply some salve on it." I started to get up, but Drake held me down.

"I'll be fine. It'll be all healed soon." He looked up at me. "I hate leaving you alone again, but if you're okay, I should go back to Castle DuMoir and check how things are going. Though, this time you should hide somewhere in the forest instead of being here alone."

I shook my head. "I'm well enough to go with you."

Drake frowned. "No, no. What if they are still fighting?"

I took his hands in mine. "All the more reason you might need me there. Besides, Morda is down. The heart is with us. All I need to do is tell the Silverblood witches to stop fighting. We can deal with the ones who don't agree with me."

It took a little more convincing and a few more words, but Drake finally relented. After I changed my shoes to sturdier ones, Thomas, Drake, and I went to Castle DuMoir.

To our surprise, the fighting had already ended—the Silverblood witches had either been killed or surrendered—but the tension was high in the air.

The dining room was crowded: Luana stood with the werewolves on one side, some of the princes stood with the vampires in the center, and Queen Sarah and Queen Rosilla were among the witches. All of them were snapping at each other, even the witches, and they seemed ready to start another fight.

Keeran saw us entering the room and rushed to us. "Thank goodness you're here. I've been trying to keep them calm, but as you can see, it's been too much."

Drake patted Keeran's shoulder.

The chattering diminished as people saw the both of us marching to the center of the room. Drake made a point of looking around, at everyone's face, showing off his power.

"I don't know about you, but I'm tired of fighting," Drake said, his voice loud and clear. The room went silent. "I know we have lots to discuss and solve, but here's what I propose we do right away: I'll take Castle DuMoir and rebuild it. I'll listen to the concerns of the vampires before finalizing a new set of rules and creating a new council."

"We don't want rules," a rebel vampire shouted from the back.

"Then you're welcome to leave right now," Drake said. "Just be sure to go far away from here, because if I catch any of you around and not following our rules, you'll be severely punished."

Murmurs rose and a handful of vampires left the room. I thought Drake would intervene and try to make them stay, but I thought I understood his main thought. Unruly vampires would only make everything difficult. I just hoped they stayed out of trouble.

"What about the witches?" Queen Sarah asked. She side-eyed me. "With your daughter being born soon, what do you suggest we do?"

Drake looked at me. "Thea should become witch queen of the Silverblood coven and the three of you—" He shifted his gaze between Queen Rosilla, Queen Sarah, and me. "—should work together to make sure the covens are united by the time our daughter comes of age and can become the Queen of All Witches."

What was he talking about? Why did he want to make me witch queen if I was about to die? We hadn't found any solution to save me. As far as I knew, I had only a month or a little over to live. If I made it to full term.

I wouldn't argue about this with him right now. Not in front of everyone.

Queen Rosilla wrinkled her nose, but nodded. "I can live with that."

"Me too," Queen Sarah said.

Drake let out a relieved sigh. "Now for the werewolves." He turned to Luana. She was wearing Keeran's leather jacket and her face looked paler than usual. "Luana is now alpha of the Dark Vale pack." Beside me, Keeran stiffened. "She'll work alongside me and Thea to maintain peace between the vampires, the witches, and the werewolves."

A couple of growls rose from the pack, but Luana growled louder, silencing them. A small smile took over my lips. It would be fun to watch her as the alpha of her pack.

For a moment, everything was perfect. Drake, Luana, Keeran, and Thomas were all right. We had defeated Morda. The princes were back and supporting Drake. The wolves looked a little tense, but I was sure they would do great under Luana's rule. As for Keeran, we still had to talk about his role in all of this. As the first male warlock allowed to co-exist with witches, we would have to come up with new rules.

I glanced around, happy our dream of a peaceful future was within reach.

Then, my happiness was shattered when my stomach tensed and pain ricocheted down my pelvis and up my back.

I tried controlling my breathing before Drake could hear it. "I'll be right back," I told him in a hush, before leaving the room.

Where I was going, what I was doing, I didn't know. I just

needed to be alone because maybe if nobody else knew about it, then it wasn't happening.

Because it was too early.

I couldn't give birth now.

23

DRAKE

THE COMMOTION CONTINUED. THE WITCHES STARTED bickering among themselves, then some wolves commented about not liking having a female for an alpha, and next everyone turned on Keeran, saying he was an aberration and we should get rid of him.

I hadn't thought leading all the groups would be easy, but I thought that everyone would take a breather before going for each other's throats again. I was just grateful there were only three races involved. I didn't want to think how messy it would be if there had been more—especially the fae, who were proud.

Thankfully, I was able to calm everyone down. I told everyone to go home—or stay in case they didn't have anywhere else to go—and rest for now. We would soon start rebuilding the castle and reorganizing our society. It wouldn't be easy. It would be stressful, actually, but it would be worth it.

The dining room cleared and I wondered where Thea had gone. She said she would be right back, so I thought she had to go to the bathroom or grab something to drink, but she hadn't come back. I was about to go look for her when Thomas appeared in front of me.

"Thank you for helping out with Morda earlier," I said.

Thomas shrugged. "I've barely done anything."

"You were there. That was enough."

He stared at me and he suddenly looked so small for a sixteen-year-old young man. "I forgive you," he blurted out. "I wanted you to know that I understand what happened and I forgive you. I still consider you my friend, my older brother."

My breath caught. "I don't deserve your forgiveness."

"Yes, you do, because I know how much guilt you feel. I know you're a good person, and I know hate when bloodlust wins over you." He sighed. "Now it's your turn to forgive yourself."

This kid ... "Thank you."

Thomas looked down. "I'm leaving."

It took a moment to sink in. "You're moving on?"

"Yes." He returned his eyes to mine. "I couldn't go before telling you. I knew I would regret it forever if I left without telling you I'd forgiven you. So now I need to go."

My eyes widened. "Now?"

He nodded. "Yes. Right now."

I reached for him. Thomas's hand became less transparent when he grabbed mine. I knew it was hard for him to keep this up for long, but I held on to him as much as I could. I shook his hand with a tight grip.

There was so much I wanted to tell him. Like how I had enjoyed our late night talks, the way he scolded me when I drank too much blood and slept on the floor, or when I came back from a mission stained in blood and dirt and didn't wash until I had drank a week's worth of blood. I wanted to tell him I had enjoyed his company and his jokes and his affection. I wanted to tell him I had been blessed for having a little brother like him.

Emotion clogged my throat and all I managed to whisper was, "Thank you."

A sad smile spread through his lips. "Take care, Drake. Please be good to Thea and your daughter."

I scoffed. "I will."

His hand became translucent. Then, the rest of his body joined in, becoming more and more transparent until there was nothing there. I waved my arms in front of me, where he had just been, and didn't touch anything.

Thomas was really gone. He had moved on. I had to be happy for him as he would finally be in peace with his parents.

"Drake!" Luana rushed back into the room.

The pitch of her voice, the rapid breathing, the speed of her heartbeat. I turned to her. "What is it?"

She stared at me with teary eyes. "It's Thea."

24

Pᴀɪɴ ᴄᴜᴛ ᴛʜʀᴏᴜɢʜ ᴍʏ ʙᴏᴅʏ, ʙᴜᴛ I ᴄᴏᴜʟᴅɴ'ᴛ ᴇᴠᴇɴ ꜱᴄʀᴇᴀᴍ.

"Hang on," Queen Sarah said.

I had tried to hang on, to delay this as much as I could, but nothing had worked. The witches had found me hiding in the garden, trying to disguise the situation. Queen Sarah and Queen Rosilla took one look at me and knew. They brought me to an empty suite in the castle and started giving orders.

"Bring towels."

"Bring water."

"Bring scissors."

"Find Drake," I croaked.

"Stay quiet," Queen Rosilla said. She put her hand on my forehead and a cold sensation spread through my face, down my neck. Her magic was almost soothing.

But then another jolt of pain ripped through me, and all I could do was grit my teeth. This wasn't a contraction; this was torture. It had to be.

"Thea, stay with us," Queen Sarah urged. "Keep your eyes open."

My eyelids were too heavy, though. My entire body was. If I didn't have this child soon, they would have to perform a C-section, because I wouldn't be awake in a few minutes.

Queen Rosilla slapped my face. "Don't you dare sleep now."

Compared to the pain on the rest of my body, the slap felt like tickles.

I groaned and widened my eyes, trying to stay awake.

The suite doors burst open. "Thea!" Drake ran to my side. He sat at the edge of the mattress and took my hand in his. "What's going on?"

"What do you think is going on?" Queen Sarah snapped. "Your daughter is about to be born."

"But ... it's too soon." His face paled. "We should have one more month at least."

"The baby wants to come now," Queen Rosilla said. "There's nothing we can do to stop her."

Drake leaned over me. "Thea ..."

I tried smiling at him, but with the pain that cut through me making me want to curl into a ball, I was sure it was more like a grimace. "It's okay, Drake. Just stay with me until the end."

Because this was the end. I could feel it. The pain was just the beginning. By all that was sacred, I hoped I could hold my daughter once before I died.

Tears filled my eyes.

"All right," Queen Sarah said. She covered my legs with a white bedsheet and took position in front of my bent knees. "Next time the pain increases, you'll push. It's gonna be a bitch, but you have to push."

I nodded, afraid of this moment. Afraid of the pain I might feel. Afraid of hurting my daughter. Afraid that I might push and die before my daughter was born. If I didn't resist until the end, the chances of her making it by herself were slim.

Queen Rosilla stood on the other side of the bed, a white towel in her hands.

The pain started in my lower back and spread down my legs, up my stomach. I gritted my teeth and pushed.

Suddenly, the world became a blur. My vision darkened until all I saw was faint silhouettes, and even the sounds faded, as if I was underwater.

"She's fading away!"

"Thea, stay with us!"

"One more push. You can do this. Just one more."

The words were a huge jumble, and it all made me more afraid.

Despite whatever they were saying, I pushed when the pain increased again, because I knew my child had to be born.

I squeezed Drake's hand hard, gritted my teeth, curled my toes, raised my shoulders, and I pushed with everything I had left.

The faint sound of crying filled my ears—the only sound I could hear.

"How is she?" Drake asked. "Is she okay?"

Queen Sarah smiled at him. "Your daughter is perfect."

All I wanted was to close my eyes and go to sleep forever, but I needed to do something first. "Give her to me," I whispered.

Queen Rosilla wrapped my daughter in the white towel and deposited her in my arms. As if she knew she was with her mommy, the baby stopped crying. Realizing I had no strength left, Drake kept his hands around mine. I hugged the bundle of warmth as tears filled my eyes. A full mop of black hair, round, rosy cheeks, and a pink pout. Even though she was small for having been born before time, she was perfect. Completely perfect.

"Hi, sweetie."

Drake kissed her forehead then mine. "I'm proud of you."

I looked from our daughter to Drake, fighting the dark dots robbing me of my sight. "I love you. Both of you."

"Don't speak like that," Queen Rosilla snapped.

"That isn't goodbye yet," Queen Sarah said.

Both queens placed their hands on my legs and sent their magic into me. I could feel it, but it was like water dripping through my fingers. It was refreshing for a second, but then it was gone. Still, they kept trying. And all it was doing was delaying the inevitable.

"Stop," I told them, my voice breaking. "It isn't working."

"We know," Queen Sarah said as she sent another jolt of magic into me. "But we have to keep trying."

"Stop," I said louder. "Please, stop."

The queens pulled back their hands.

"Thea, please," Drake whispered. "Don't give up yet."

I didn't want to give up, but I also couldn't hang on anymore. I was fading too fast, and I wanted to tell him goodbye before I left for good.

A tear rolled down my cheek. "It's okay," I lied. I wasn't okay with this. I wanted to live a long life with the man I loved and my sweet daughter. I wanted to teach her magic and see her grow into her powers and become a great, fair Queen of All Witches.

Drake wiped the tear from my face. "Don't leave us."

What did he want me to say to that?

My vision darkened more and my head spun. I was losing the fight.

I placed a soft kiss on our daughter's cheek. "Please, take good care of her." I pressed my lips to his.

"Fight this, Thea," Drake said, his voice breaking. "Please, keep fighting."

I laid my head on his shoulder and closed my eyes, trusting he would catch our daughter when my arms failed.

The doors burst open a second time. "Wait!" a new voice shouted. "Thea, hang on."

"You!" Queen Rosilla said.

"I can't believe it," Queen Sarah said.

I blinked, trying to focus my sight. "Who is it?"

"It's me," the newcomer said. I blinked again and finally saw her. Bagatha stood beside Drake. "I think we can save you."

Drake's arms tensed. "What? How?"

She glanced at him. "Do you still have the Blood Amulet?"

He pulled the pendant from under his shirt. "Here."

"And the heart of the Silverblood coven?"

"In my pocket," I rasped.

Queen Sarah took it from my pocket.

"Good. Now follow my instructions," Bagatha said. Her wand appeared in her hand and she placed it on my chest. "Set the Blood Amulet and the coven heart with my wand." Queen Rosilla took my daughter from me. I didn't want to let her go, but there was no strength in my arms. Like a good student, Drake did what Bagatha said. "Say these words out loud." She showed him a ripped yellowed paper. "Then cut your palm and drip some of your blood on the wand, the heart, the amulet, and in Thea's mouth."

My stomach tightened. "W-what?"

"Just do it," Bagatha urged.

Without hesitation, Drake followed her instructions. He rested the pulsing heart and the cold Blood Amulet on my chest. Next, he took out his dagger from the strap on his leg and cut his palm—a big gash. Blood oozed from his wound down to the heart and the amulet. Then he brought his hand to my mouth.

I clamped my lips.

"Thea, please, just drink it."

I stared at Bagatha. "You're not turning me into a vampire, are you?"

"No, dear," she said. "I promise."

Reluctantly, I opened my mouth. Drake squeezed his wound and blood filled my mouth. Bile rose in my throat, but I swallowed the blood before I could throw up.

"What now?" Drake asked.

"Just give it some time to work," Bagatha said.

Still feeling like I could sleep for a thousand years, I closed my eyes and rested my head on Drake's shoulder again.

"Stay awake, Thea," he whispered. A few seconds passed and he spoke louder, "It isn't working."

"It should," Bagatha said, sounding sure.

Well, it wasn't. I felt the darkness coming, wrapping its thick arms around me, and cradling me, taking me away to its lair.

Until a jolt of energy cut through me, bringing in an explosion of light.

I jerked and gasped for air, as if I had been underwater for too long.

"Thea? Talk to me!" Drake held my shoulders.

Slowly, I sat up and opened my eyes. I took a moment to analyze how I felt. No darkness, no dizziness, no weakness. I hadn't felt this energized and strong in months, even before I found out I was pregnant.

"I feel great." I lifted my arms and looked down at my hands. My magic tingled under my skin, ready to be called upon. "My magic is back."

"Thank goodness." Drake cupped my hand and glued his lips to mine. With a huge, dazzling smile, he looked at Bagatha. "What was that? How did you find it?"

I beckoned for Queen Rosilla and she handed my daughter back to me. I cradled my baby, as tight as I could without hurting her, as emotion filled my chest. I was alive. I felt great. And I was holding a perfectly beautiful and healthy daughter.

Bagatha smiled at us. "After I told you about the Immortal Vow and how there was no way of saving Thea, I started my own research." I remembered Drake saying he had visited Bagatha a couple of times to check if she had found anything. "But in the past month, I have visited several witch covens in a handful of countries. I talked to their queens and councils, searched their libraries and grimoires, until I found the oldest witch queen I had ever met. Queen Neith from the Blacklotus coven in Egypt is over six thousand years old. She has thousands of grimoires with every kind of spell you can imagine, and most of those spells were invented by her. Queen Neith didn't have a specific spell to save Thea, so she made up one."

Drake's jaw hit the floor. "Are you saying it could have *not* worked?"

"Queen Neith is confident in her abilities," Bagatha said. "According to her, all of her spells have worked so far."

"Thank you," I said. Tears brimmed in my eyes again. "You went to great lengths to save me, and you didn't have to."

She scoffed. "Of course I had to. You're the mother of my successor." She smiled at my daughter. "I know witches aren't the motherly kind, but I had a feeling you're about to change that, and I didn't want to deprive this little girl from having her mother beside her."

Drake smiled at her. "Thank you."

"Oh, one bit of information before I let you rest," Bagatha said. "This spell used the magic of the Blood Amulet and the Silverblood's heart, plus the remainder of my magic imbued to my wand, to link both of your lives." I frowned. "Which means, it is Drake's life force that sustains you now, Thea. You'll live as long as he lives."

Drake's eyes widened. "You're saying Thea is immortal now?"

She grinned. "That's exactly what I'm saying."

Drake turned his bright green eyes to me. I knew he had been worried about that since the beginning of our relationship. I had no desire to become a vampire, but that meant I would one day die and he would be alone. But now, I could still be a simple witch and live with him forever. The relief was stamped in his handsome face.

Queen Sarah cleared her throat. "Did you say you put all of your magic in that wand, Bagatha?"

The old witch grabbed the wand and snapped it, breaking it in half like a useless little twig. "Yes. And it's all gone now."

"That's crazy," Queen Sarah barked.

Bagatha grabbed the queen's arm. "Thea and the baby need to rest now. We can talk about this outside."

Queen Rosilla followed them to the door. She said, "Call us if you need anything," before exiting the room and closing the door behind them.

Drake embraced our daughter and me. "I don't think I could be happier."

"Me neither," I confessed. I looked down at our baby. "We still haven't named her."

"She'll be known in the entire supernatural world. We should choose a strong name for her."

I stared at the sleeping bug in my arms. I couldn't believe I had just escaped death and was now destined to live forever with the man I loved and my powerful daughter. Life was too perfect and I had never felt this happy.

"I have an idea," I said.

"Tell me."

I smiled. "Her name will be Aurora."

25

DRAKE

I KNELT IN FRONT OF AURORA AND TIGHTENED THE BOW around her waist. "Are you ready?"

Aurora blinked at me before smiling and spinning around, showing off her white dress. She tripped on her feet and I put my hand out in case she fell. For a one year old, Aurora had a great balance already. She hadn't been walking for two months, but now she wanted to run and jump and monkey around.

Today though she wanted to dance, mostly, and it was all because of the pretty white dress and the flowers weaved into her short hair. Sometimes I stared at her, amazed at the little beautiful miracle she was. She had my black hair, but Thea's fair complexion, her tiny nose, and her pretty gray eyes. I could see her breaking a lot of hearts when older—and I was not prepared for that.

Pushing those thoughts away, I stood and tightened my tie. I had no idea why I was suddenly so nervous. It wasn't as if I hadn't seen everyone in the next room before.

When I offered, Aurora slipped her little hand into mine. I opened the door and together, we entered the room.

In the year since the DuMoir battle, all the races had worked together. The vampires helped rebuild DuMoir Castle. The Silverblood witches returned to their manor on the Silverblood estate. The Blackmarsh and the Bluemoon witches also went back to their covens, but kept in touch often.

Thea and Aurora lived with me at DuMoir Castle, but since Thea was the witch queen of the Silverblood coven, she stopped there at least once a week to make sure everything was okay. While she wasn't there, Elisa was in command—a young Silverblood witch who had proven herself to us in the last year.

Keeran also lived in the castle with us. His real place in our society was still unknown as most of the witches weren't willing to accept him—but they didn't dare touch him since he had Thea's protection.

Luana had gone back to her pack. Despite the tough front she put up most of time, she had expressed her concern over her power to Thea and me many times. Apparently, most of the male wolves didn't want a female as their alpha. Thankfully, none had acted against her yet.

Despite all the tension we still encounter, the reconstructed ballroom was now full with our friends and the most important figures in our society. Queen Rosilla, Queen Sarah, and their councils. Luana and a dozen of her wolves. All of the Silverblood witches. Keeran and Bagatha. We had also invited the faes and other supernaturals, but hadn't heard back from them.

Our guests occupied the chairs spread over the floor and

turned to look at Aurora and me as we walked down the aisle in the middle of the room.

My daughter and I stopped at the bottom of the stairs, where Keeran waited for us. He looked regal in black tuxedo, and a dark red tie.

Aurora hugged his legs and Keeran smiled at her.

I looked out to the doors at the end of the ballroom and shifted my weight.

"Are you nervous?" Keeran asked in a low voice. In a room full of supernaturals, I was sure at least a handful had heard him. "Lord Drake is nervous. I didn't think I would ever see the day."

"Shut the hell up," I muttered.

He chuckled.

A moment later, the doors opened and my breath caught.

Smiling, Thea walked into the room and I was damn sure I had never seen a more beautiful sight in my entire long life. Her long, blond hair was tied into a thick braid over her shoulder, showing off her perfect face and delicate makeup— except for her blood red lips. Her off-white dress was tight around her chest and waist, but it flared up around her hips, where pieces of off-white lace created a skirt that went down to the floor. Lace covered her collarbone and shoulders. In her hands, she held a bouquet of dark red roses.

With each passing day, I was convinced I loved her more and more.

The guests whispered as she walked past them.

"She's so beautiful."

"Love her dress."

"She's a real queen."

"Drake is a lucky man."

When Thea was close enough, I took a step toward her

and offered her my arm. Smiling at me, she took my arm. My chest constricted with pure love.

Thea and I faced Keeran. Aurora played around us while Keeran married Thea and me.

A wedding seemed silly for supernaturals. We didn't have any specific religion, and we couldn't register our marriage in any town, but I thought it would be a great way of celebrating all we had accomplished since Thea and I met. After many ups and downs, we had made it. We were together, loving each other, and we had managed to bring the vampires, the witches, and the werewolves together.

I couldn't think of any way better to celebrate then to pledge my love to the woman who had robbed my dead heart in front of everyone we knew.

After the ceremony, the chairs were pulled to the perimeter of the ballroom, where tables awaited with silverware and drinks. Soon, dinner was served, complete with dessert and blood, and then the party started.

Three songs in, Aurora fell asleep in Luana's arms.

Seven songs in, my wife made me a proposition I couldn't resist. We sneaked out of the ballroom and raced to our chambers.

Thankfully, no one was here at this time. Once we stepped inside, I locked the door and hovered over Thea.

With her eyes on mine, she reached for her waist. Then, she unhooked her skirt. It fell to the floor and I stared at her long legs. The bodice of her dress didn't actually end at her hips. It went down to her thighs, like a shorter dress. Right now, I kind of loved that dress.

"Kiss me," she whispered.

26

THEA

"Kiss me," I whispered, my head in a daze.

Drake didn't waste a second. He stepped into me, and pressing me against the door with his palms flat against the wood, caging me in, he kissed me. His lips were warm and soft and made of pure ecstasy. I melted into his kiss, parting my lips for him. His tongue sneaked in, teasing mine and ripping a moan from my throat.

He groaned, taking my lower lip between his teeth. "Delicious," he whispered, before taking my mouth again. His hands slid down my waist, down to my thighs, leaving a trail of fire across my body, and all I could do was moan in his mouth.

He hooked his fingers under the hem of my dress and teased my skin. I gasped, sinking my nails into his shoulders. He groaned again, before splaying his big hands on the back of my thighs and tugging on them. My mind on a cloud of pure delight, I let him pull my legs up, and I was half conscious as I wrapped them around his waist. He thrust his hips against mine, rubbing his hard on against me. I moaned again.

His lips trailed down my jaw, and paused at my neck. His elaborated breathing was all I could hear as he thrust his hips into mine again. Helpless, I moaned once more.

"Hell, these little sounds ..." He nicked at the tip of my ear, then slid his hands to my hips and pulled me up against him.

I let out a surprised yelp as he crossed the room and deposited me on a large dining table. Sliding his hot hands over my skin, he pushed my dress up until it bunched at my waist, revealing my lace panties.

I didn't have time to be think as Drake pressed his hard on against my center, and I wished my panties would melt away. But then, he let out a hiss and hooked his fingers on the lacy top of my dress. He reached back and undid the buttons, then tugged it down, just enough to give him access to my cleavage.

Drake dipped his head and ran his tongue over the top arch of my breast. My lips parted, I wrapped my arms around his neck and arched my back. Right now, I would do anything he wanted.

He kept playing with his tongue, running it around my breast until, finally, he flicked my nipples. I bucked, wishing he was inside me. He closed his mouth around my breast, and I melted some more. By all that was sacred, how could it feel this good? Was he feeling what I was feeling? Did he want me as much as I wanted him?

One of his hands snaked up, wrapping around my free breast. He pinched my hardened nipples and I bucked again. Pure heat and pleasure swam through me, and I wanted more, more, more.

Feeling bold and sexy, I slid my hands over his chest and found the hem of his shirt. While savoring each lap of his tongue and suck of his mouth, I explored his stomach and chest, always in awe of the many muscles under his warm skin.

He pushed his hips against me again—I shivered.

Biting my lower lip, I undid the button and zipper of his pants, and slipped my hand inside his pants. He hissed, his teeth gently closing around my nipples as I ran my hand over his massive hard on.

Loving the way he reacted to my touch, I moved my hand up and down, up and down, pushing hard against his shaft. Drake shivered, then he grabbed my wrists, and pulled my hands away.

Straightening, he looked at me. "Keep that up and I won't last."

He leaned into me and captured my mouth again. I surrendered to the kiss, melting into his arms, being sucked from reality, and loving every second of it. I tightened my legs around him and, with my feet, tugged him to me. He let out a small chuckle against my lips as he obliged and thrust his hips on mine, rubbing his hard on against my center. Breaking the kiss, I threw my head back. Drake's lips found my neck and he switched between kissing and grazing his fangs at my delicate skin.

He grabbed hold of my shoulders and pushed me down, until my back was flat on the table. Then he knelt in front of me.

I sucked in a sharp breath.

Drake slipped off my panties with ease, then trailed small pecks from my ankle, up my knees, to the inside of my thigh. I tensed in anticipation, and my hands flew to his silky hair.

He licked my center, and with a loud gasp, my hips bucked and my back arched off the table.

"Hell, you taste so good," he whispered, before flicking his tongue over my clit again.

Then he slipped a finger inside me. Then a second one. I slapped my hands on the table and curled my fingers around the edge, trying to hold on before I lost it. Before I melted away. Before the pleasure took over and I became a useless pile of pure bliss.

He pumped his fingers inside me, fucking me with his hand, hard and deep. He sucked on my clit, hard, and I was done for. Pleasure exploded inside me, sending me in a spiral of heat and bliss. With a low chuckle, Drake licked my center one more time, then stood straight. My mind was a beautiful haze, but I couldn't stop looking at him, gawking at the handsome man before me. He was mine, all mine, for all eternity.

Grabbing my hips, Drake pushed inside me in one quick, fast thrust. I cried as he filled me. Damn, he was too much, too big, too hard, too ... everything.

In a slow rhythm, pulling out and pushing back in in slow, long thrusts, Drake worked me up. The pressure built up again, but it was different this time. Deeper, more powerful.

"Hell," Drake hissed. "This is too good."

With swift movements, Drake pulled out his shirt, wrapped an arm under my back, and pulled me up, so I was seated up on the table, my breasts pressed tight against his bare chest. He leaned into me and captured my mouth, just as his movements sped and he pushed inside me fast, deep, and hard.

I gasped against his mouth and that only seemed to entice

him more. Holding on to me, Drake pumped into my core, drawing out the hidden fire I had only known with him.

Breaking the skin, I stretched my neck. Instantly, his fangs elongated and he licked his lips.

"I know you want it," I rasped.

He didn't hesitate. Drake sank his teeth on my neck and drank my blood. Like magic, the desire inside me increased tenfold, and I couldn't help but moan. Holding me tight, he groaned, as if he couldn't get enough—of my blood and me.

A wave of pure heat rolled through me, and I sank my nails on Drake's back, stilling for a moment, before the fire burst and I melted away in little quivers.

Drake groaned and pulled his head back. He returned his lips to mine. He kissed me hard and deep as he pushed into me hard once, twice, three times, then broke out in little trembles.

"Holy hell," he whispered, leaning his heavy body over mine.

I know, I wanted to tell him, but my mouth couldn't catch up with my dazed brain and numb body.

After a moment, Drake scooped me up and took me to our bed. He gently laid me down and stared at me, his green eyes full of desire.

"Someone looks ready for round two," I teased.

He lay on top of me, pressing his hard body on mine. "This is our wedding night, my love. We need to break some sort of record." I chuckled. But instead of going for it, Drake nestled his face on my neck and inhaled deeply. "I'm happy right here, like this."

I wound my arms around his neck and held on tight. "Me too."

He pulled back a little and stared at me. "I'm proud of us."

We had come a long way, hadn't we? All that we had gone through since we first met ... I sometimes looked back and wondered how we did it. If I were to go back in time, I felt like I wouldn't be able to accomplish the same. I wouldn't have been strong enough. But then again, maybe I would. After all, I had Drake by my side and I was sure I could face anything, any hardship, as long as he held my hand.

I smiled at him. "Me too."

Life was far from being perfect, and there were many issues with the supernaturals we still had to fix, but right now? Right now, everything was perfect.

And it would be perfect for as long as we lived.

Forever.

Thea's and Drake's story has come to an end, but you can start reading Keeran's and Luana's story now! *The Warlock Lord*, book 4 in the Rite World universe!

THANK YOU

ABOUT THE AUTHOR

While USA Today Bestselling Author Juliana Haygert dreams of being Wonder Woman, Buffy, or a blood elf shadow priest, she settles for the less exciting—but equally gratifying—life as a wife, a mother, and an author. She resides in North Carolina and spends her days writing about kick-ass heroines and the heroes who drive them crazy.

Subscribe to her mailing list to receive emails of announcement, events, and other fun stuff related to her writing and her books: www.bit.ly/JuHNL

For more information:
www.julianahaygert.com

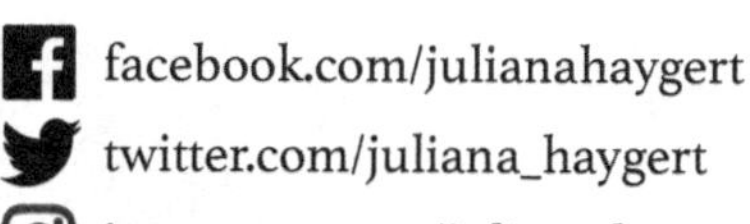

facebook.com/julianahaygert

twitter.com/juliana_haygert

instagram.com/juliana.haygert

ALSO BY JULIANA HAYGERT

To find links and more info, go to:

www.julianahaygert.com/books/

Free

Into the Darkest Fire

Tested

Rite World: Blackthorn Hunters Academy

The Demon Kiss (Book 1)

The Hunter Secret (Book 2)

The Soul Bond (Book 3)

The Shadow Trials (Book 4)

The Infernal Curse (Book 5)

Rite World

The Vampire Heir (Book 1)

The Witch Queen (Book 2)

The Immortal Vow (Book 3)

The Warlock Lord (Book 4)

The Wolf Consort (Book 5)

The Crystal Rose (Book 6)

The Wolf Forsaken (Book 7)

The Fae Bound (Book 8)

The Blood Pact (Book 9)

The Fire Heart Chronicles

Heart Seeker (Book 1)

Flame Caster (Book 2)

Sorrow Bringer (Book 3)

Earth Shaker (Novella)

Soul Wanderer (Book 4)

Fate Summoner (Book 5)

War Maiden (Book 6)

The Everlast Series

Destiny Gift (Book 1)

Soul Oath (Book 2)

Cup of Life (Book 3)

Everlasting Circle (Book 4)

Willow Harbor Series

Hunter's Revenge (Book 3)

Siren's Song (Book 5)

Breaking Series

Breaking Free (Book 1)

Breaking Away (Book 2)

Breaking Through (Book 3)

Breaking Down (Book 4)